"It was just a kiss."

"It wasn't 'just' anything, sweetheart." Justin turned his head toward Olivia, his eyes erotically intense. "And try looking at it from the other side, if you don't believe me," he continued. "Are you honestly saying you couldn't make a few educated guesses about my performance now?"

Flames licked through her blood. On the job, her vibrant visualization skills served her well, but all they were helping with now was raising the temperature inside the car. *Justin sliding the straps of her bra down her shoulders, kissing her exposed skin... lowering her to a mattress, covering her body with his weight...kissing her as she straddled him...*

Olivia wanted to tell him that his *performance* was none of her concern. But if she opened her mouth to speak, the words *take me* would spill out of their own volition.

Dear Reader,

I can't tell you how many times I've decided on a clear plan, only to have it go...well, *kablooey* is the word that springs to mind. Cartoonlike, but accurate. Has this ever happened to you? It's about to happen to Olivia Lockhart and Justin Hawthorne.

With a recent breakup behind her, Olivia has vowed not to repeat her past romantic mistakes. She's going to find someone more stable than sexy and more interested in committing than flirting—despite her attraction to irresistible photographer Justin Hawthorne. Justin, who finished raising his sisters after his parents' deaths, has just seen his youngest sister off to college and has resolved to reclaim his bachelor freedom—which does not include settling down with one woman. But the best-laid plans are no match for love!

I hope you enjoy Justin and Olivia's story. I love entertaining readers, and I also love hearing from them. You can write me at t.michaels@earthlink.net or visit my Web site at www.tanyamichaels.com for information on giveaways and upcoming releases.

Wishing you plans that go smoothly, or at least plenty of laughter when they don't!

Tanya Michaels

Books by Tanya Michaels

HARLEQUIN TEMPTATION
968—HERS FOR THE WEEKEND
HARLEQUIN FLIPSIDE
6—WHO NEEDS DECAF?
HARLEQUIN DUETS
96—THE MAID OF DISHONOR

TANYA MICHAELS

SHEER DECADENCE

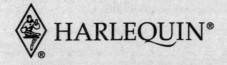

TORONTO • NEW YORK • LONDON
AMSTERDAM • PARIS • SYDNEY • HAMBURG
STOCKHOLM • ATHENS • TOKYO • MILAN • MADRID
PRAGUE • WARSAW • BUDAPEST • AUCKLAND

For Rachelle Wadsworth, Dorene Graham
and Anna DeStefano. Thank you for all the feedback,
support, brainstorming
and just plain fun!

ISBN 0-373-69186-6

SHEER DECADENCE

Copyright © 2004 by Tanya Michna.

This edition published by arrangement with Harlequin Books S.A.

® and TM are trademarks of the publisher. Trademarks indicated with
® are registered in the United States Patent and Trademark Office, the
Canadian Trade Marks Office and in other countries.

www.eHarlequin.com

Printed in U.S.A.

"But did I tell you what he *said* after I found him in bed with my roommate?" Olivia Lockhart sat behind her oak desk, scowling at the three-week-old memory of Sean's parting words. "He said 'Babe, when a man's as in demand as I am, it wouldn't be fair to the women of the world to limit myself to just one.' I am finished with smooth-talking, good-looking men."

Was early March way too late to add a New Year's resolution?

Jeanie, the office receptionist who stood leaning against Olivia's file cabinet, wrinkled her pixie features into an uncharacteristic grimace. "So you're going out with ugly men now?"

They were probably more faithful. "I don't plan on seeing anyone for a while."

Olivia had spent her dateless high-school years with homemade brownies and her mom's old Cary Grant movies. Now, she had plenty of dates, but she'd been better off with Cary and the brownies. In fact, if she could find a decent brownie that didn't go straight to her hips, maybe she could give up men all together.

"If you don't date, what will you *do?*" Jeanie's distressed tone made such an existence sound unthinkable. For her, it probably was.

With her heart-shaped face and ultrashort platinum

hair, adorably petite Jeanie looked like head cheer-leader for Santa's elves and had the bubbly personality to match. Men flocked to her, but she'd been pretty serious about the same guy, Albert, for the last few months. Olivia had high hopes for them. She had to have hope for someone.

"I have plenty to keep me busy," Olivia said. "Friends, work. You know I want to be named Design Supervisor."

Jeanie narrowed her brown eyes. "Are you sure you're not just saying that because you're gun-shy?"

"I'm sure." Getting promoted had been Olivia's real New Year's resolution. When she'd been younger, she'd made up for romantic failures by excelling in school. Now, she'd apply the extra energy to her job until she could figure out how to improve her luck with men.

"Because I'd hate to see you cheat yourself out of The One just because of Sean," Jeanie continued. "Albert has an older brother, and I'd be happy to set you up. He really likes exotic-looking women."

Suppressing startled laughter, Olivia leaned back in her chair. "Exotic?"

"Well, you're so tall, and you have all that long black hair. Gives you a mysterious aura."

"Ah." As far as she could tell, the only mystery in her life was her track record of bad relationship decisions. She was an otherwise competent woman. "Thanks anyway, Jeanie. If he's Albert's brother, I'm sure he's wonderful, but I'm putting romance on the back burner for a while."

"But—"

"Maybe we can discuss this later." Olivia glanced down at the proofs for next month's catalog on her cluttered desk. "I have a ton of work."

With a nod and one last sympathetic glance, Jeanie scampered out of the office. The smaller woman often made Olivia feel like an Amazon; today Jeanie left her feeling old and cynical, too. Hard to believe only four years separated her from the twenty-two-year-old receptionist.

Pushing away thoughts of her co-worker, Olivia told herself to focus. She really did have a lot to do. Mondays were always jam-packed, full of new tasks as well as remaining errands that hadn't been quite finished the week before.

The piles on her desk were organized by "Can put off," "Must finish or I can't go home today," and "So long overdue I don't even remember what needed to be done with it." And those stacks threatened to grow even larger with the company's expansion. Sweet Nothings, an Atlanta-based lingerie catalog had started as a strictly mail-order business, but with increased presence at fashion shows and a tremendously successful Web site, preparations were being made to open brick-and-mortar stores.

To increase buzz, corporate management had asked Olivia's boss, Steve Reynolds, to bring in a second full-time photographer and begin planning the first ever Sweet Nothings calendar. Until now, their on-staff photographer, Fred, had handled the workload with the help of some freelancers, but Sweet Nothings was evolving every day. Olivia just hoped an upcoming promotion to Design Supervisor would be part of that evolution.

Seeking inspiration for all that remained to be done for the current issue, she thumbed through the catalog that had come out in December. She stopped on a glossy page featuring their most popular model, blond statuesque Stormy, in a lacy negligee.

Looking for something more effective than mistletoe this holiday season? Try surprising him in our burgundy silk... The text went on to detail make, fit and care of the garment, but all any man would care about was the fastest way to get the woman out of it.

Reminding herself that many women bought lingerie for the express purpose of having it removed, she told herself not to be bitter. Her bad mood was ironic since, as a teenager in what her mother had injudiciously dubbed the "ugly duckling period," Olivia would have thought a single date with a gorgeous worldly man like Sean would translate to infinite bliss. *Ha.* She wasn't sure they'd achieved bliss, but whatever they'd shared, it had definitely been finite.

Next time she met a man who seemed too good to be true, she should keep in mind he probably was. *You're too easily seduced.* Not in the literal sense, but seduced by the romantic fantasies she'd built up during her wallflower years.

Prior to high school, Olivia had been taller than all but a few boys in her class, and had outweighed many of them. It wasn't until college, when she'd taken every athletic elective her marketing degree allowed and walked several miles a day just to get around campus, that the last of her "baby fat" had really melted away.

By graduation, the only area of her body she hadn't been able to slenderize was her chest, but men didn't seem to mind.

Since nothing could be done about her height, she tried to use it to her advantage, projecting confidence she didn't always feel, a confidence that was at first bolstered by a dramatic increase in dates. It had been exciting to go to clubs on the arms of attractive men and, though the feminist in her cringed to admit it, validating. Too bad so many of her boyfriends had turned out to be jerks—Sean being the most recent in a parade of romantic mistakes.

The breakup, paired with her ethics-free roommate moving out and leaving Olivia to cover both halves of the rent, made this the perfect time to concentrate on becoming Design Supervisor. The promotion would include a raise and a much-coveted corner office. She'd been assigned more responsibilities lately, including her first supervisory role on an upcoming shoot, and she knew she was being tested. Maybe if she got the promotion, she'd dip her toes back into the dating pool, but when she did, she'd find someone nice and reliable, not another sexy playboy heavy on charm and light on scruples.

A knock against the open door startled her—people bucking for advancement shouldn't be caught staring into space—and she jerked her head up to find a golden Adonis of a man leaning against the doorjamb. His eyes were a clear jewel-tone green, and his face was flawless, with a strong square jaw and chiseled cheekbones. Very tall, he had the kind of broad shoulders that would photograph equally well bare-chested or in a tuxedo shot.

Hardly the first time an incredibly attractive man had appeared in her doorway. Of course, they showed up at 461 when what they really wanted was 416. Story of her life.

"Male models should check in with Meg Jansen," she told him. "Office 416, on the other side of the elevators."

He arched a dark blond eyebrow in surprise. "Male models? I wasn't looking for Meg Jansen. I wanted Olivia—" he consulted the yellow sticky-note in his hand "—Lockhart. Is that you?"

"Y-yes. And you are?"

"Justin Hawthorne," he introduced himself. "Your photographer for the South Carolina shoot."

This paragon of masculine appeal? No, no, no. "I believe Fred Elliot is my photographer for our swimwear issue." She and grizzled veteran Fred already had a solid working relationship, had brainstormed locations and concepts often.

"Sorry, with Fred's sister sick in Cincinnati, they substituted me for Stormy's swimsuit shoot." Justin grinned. "Try saying *that* three times fast."

In addition to an obvious sense of humor, he had a great smile. Perfect even white teeth. A half dimple to the left of his mouth.

You are not going to notice his mouth.

Too late.

"I wanted to drop by and introduce myself before the meeting this afternoon," he told her. "Steve just hired me away from Hilliard High Life, the sporting goods line for the ski-lodge and country-club set.''

She nodded to indicate familiarity with Hilliard's catalog, but she'd only partially heard everything after *hired.* She'd assumed Justin was one of the freelancers, not realizing Steve had made a final decision.

"Don't worry," Justin added. "I've got plenty of experience, so you'll be in good hands.''

The thought of being in his experienced hands made her mouth go dry. "Um...right, okay.''

He glanced past her shoulder at the bold painting that hung behind her desk. "Interesting.''

She followed his gaze. Her original Kallie Carmichael had been a gift to herself when she'd received her very first promotion at Sweet Nothings, graduating from copywriter to the layout team. The obscure artist's use of bright colors and odd abstract visuals drew mixed reactions. Olivia wondered if Justin, as Sean first had, would pretend to like it in order to impress her.

"What do you think?'' she asked.

"I'm not wild about it.''

Well, if he hadn't appreciated Kallie's brilliant work, at least he'd been honest.

"I much prefer Ms. Carmichael's later pieces,'' he added. "Particularly the series in green she called Rebirth.''

She blinked. "You know who Kallie Carmichael is?''

His grin widened. "Did you think you were her only fan?''

What she thought was that Justin Hawthorne had one of the best smiles she'd ever seen.

When she couldn't form an immediate answer, he

nodded a quick goodbye. "See you at this afternoon's meeting."

Once he'd gone, Olivia exhaled in frustration and self-disgust. There was no good reason for her mind to have gone blank and her pulse to have jumped. Yes, he was incredible-looking, but so what? Her last boyfriend had been a model, and a very clear lesson that the insides weren't always as attractive as the outside suggested.

Still, something about Justin... *Don't think of him as Justin. Think of him as Mr. Hawthorne. Or the photographer. Or even "that guy."* The less personal, the better.

They did have something in common, though. While she hadn't been able to afford any of the paintings, Rebirth was a favorite series of hers, too. But shared admiration of an artist was no reason to lust after a coworker she hardly knew. Co-worker. She clung to the steadying reminder that they'd be working together.

Securing her promotion required consummate professionalism, not drooling over J—that guy.

STACCATO high-heeled footsteps and accompanying feminine voices passed through the hall outside the Human Resources office, where Justin was completing personnel paperwork. One woman laughed, and the unabashed husky sound held just the right note of mischief to pique his interest. She sounded like someone who knew how to have fun.

Turning in his chair, he glanced through the open door and did a double take when he saw Olivia Lockhart. She stood waiting for the elevator with an attractive black woman, chuckling at something her friend had said. *So much for first impressions.*

When Olivia had first looked up at him this morning, he'd experienced a slash of desire—her clear gray eyes were a striking contrast to her jet-black hair and full red lips—but as beautiful as she was, she'd also seemed aloof. He'd wondered at the time if Olivia was always so withdrawn, or if she'd objected to something about him specifically. She certainly didn't seem withdrawn now.

Her quick grin and earthy laugh heightened the attraction he'd felt earlier, and he watched her enter the elevator, appreciating the way her dark skirt hugged shapely hips. Between his line of work and having two younger sisters, Justin had run into a number of females who were dedicated to the pursuit of a stick figure. Personally, Justin liked women who were shaped like women. Olivia's curves were damn near perfect.

"Almost finished?" The assistant HR manager, Kate Ames, tugged his thoughts away from Olivia and back to work. A young brunette with wavy hair and a bright smile, Kate had been nothing but friendly.

He nodded. "Just about."

Two questions left, and he'd be a certified employee of Sweet Nothings. Excitement pulsed through him, not just because of the job—although what was not to love about photographing lingerie models?—but because of what this career change represented. For almost seven years, he'd dutifully put his wants and needs, from occupational choices to his love life, on hold. He'd taken on responsibilities he'd never expected, but now it was time to reclaim his life, be a little selfish. To begin with, he'd make up for the too many nights he'd slept alone. There were dozens of hot women out there, and he wanted to meet as many of them as possible.

Still, despite his enthusiasm over the new job, he had trouble refocusing on his paperwork. Which was the real Olivia: the coolly contained woman he'd encountered earlier, or the woman he'd watched in the hall, the one with the hint of wickedness in her laugh?

"I DON'T KNOW how you do it," Meg Jansen said.

Ignoring the enticing scent of her friend's French fries, Olivia picked at her salad. "If you'd seen me in high school, you'd know how I do it." The willpower had been hard-earned, but worth it.

This is what's wrong with my love life. Outside of finally ending a long-standing affair with Ben and Jerry, when it came to men, Olivia hadn't found the self-discipline to replace the decadent with the nutritious. Men like Sean fell into the "dessert" category—no matter how tempting they were, they weren't healthy in the long run.

Meg shook her head sadly. "All your attention to a well-balanced diet and getting up every morning to jog...that can't be good for you." Though Meg's own curves ran toward the ample side, she was beautiful, dark-skinned with a close cap of short curls that accentuated her high cheekbones and wide hazel eyes, and she was at ease with her body in a way Olivia envied.

"No fries," her friend continued. "Never any dessert. You don't smoke. Jeanie says now no men, either?

Tell me you have some vice I don't know about, or I'm gonna worry about you just snapping one day."

"So if I said I was a shopaholic, or drank martinis every afternoon, you'd feel better?"

"Much. Repression is not healthy."

"Martinis are?"

"Maybe, maybe not...let's discuss it over a round of drinks."

Olivia laughed. "I'd love to, but this afternoon is one of Steve's meetings."

"In that case, we'd better order *two* rounds. Honest to God, that man can talk longer and say less than anyone I've ever met." Meg swabbed another fry through ketchup. "Are you really going on a no-men kick?"

A kick that would be easier to uphold without Justin Hawthorne around. His smile had been plaguing her all morning. Okay, his smile *and* the first-rate buns she'd ogled when he'd turned and left her office.

"Not forever. And I'm not giving up all men, just a certain type. Sean lasted longer than the guy before him, but in the end..." Olivia speared a crouton on her fork with a crunch.

She wouldn't say she was *broken*hearted, exactly; the sting of finding Sean in bed with Candace had been more like a deep and unexpected paper cut. But the humiliation alone was something she'd never wish on another person, the embarrassment of having wrongly trusted, the paranoia of wondering how long it had been going on and whether or not they'd laughed at her.

If she hadn't loved Sean, she'd at least thought they were working toward that possibility. During their six months together, his publicly flirtatious manner had sometimes bothered her, but he'd said it was just part of his professional persona. So she'd ignored her instincts, swayed by the argument that she was misjudging him based on previous bad apples. Turned out he was a lot like other McIntoshes and Granny Smiths she'd known.

Well, no man was making a fool of her again.

"You're better off without him," Meg said quietly.

"Hey, I'm just glad it happened when it did. A couple days later, I wouldn't have been able to return his Valentine's Day gift for a full refund."

Meg ignored the attempted joke. "Not all men are like that."

But I pick the ones who are. "Right, and I'm going to look for a completely different type of man. Just not yet. You know I want the design promotion, so as soon as I get back from vacation—"

"The doomed vacation?"

"Not doomed, postponed."

Originally, Olivia and Sean had planned to go to the remote Pacific island resort of Kaokara together, but had rescheduled because he'd been sick. When she thought of how she'd taken the rat fink her homemade chicken noodle soup.... Olivia had been forced to reschedule *again* when a last-minute crisis arose at work. Now she planned to take the trip alone, needing the tropical rest and relaxation more than ever.

"I reconfirmed my flight this morning. The minute that shoot in South Carolina is wrapped up, I am out of here." Mentioning the beach assignment reminded

Olivia of the startling switch in photographers. "Hey, did you know Fred's sister was sick?"

"I heard she needs an operation. Her prognosis is great, but Fred's going down for a little while to help with her kids. What brought that up?"

"The new photographer, Justin Hawthorne. He's being officially introduced at the meeting this afternoon. He dropped by my office earlier to let me know he's going with me Wednesday. Met him yet?"

"Nope, I was tied up on the phone all morning with modeling agencies. Is he anything like Fred?"

"They could not be more different." Unfortunately. "I mistook him for one of your guys gone astray."

Meg arched an eyebrow. "He's as attractive as our male models?"

Better. "Close enough."

"Oh, good, new eye candy!" Meg leaned back with a grin. "Maybe this afternoon's meeting won't be so boring after all."

Not sharing her friend's enthusiasm, Olivia smiled weakly. After a brief dating fast, she was going to change her ways—stop dating yummy heartbreakers and find a nice reliable man and a healthy relationship, the romantic equivalent of salad. She didn't need the temptation of walking pieces of chocolate like Justin Hawthorne.

2

OLIVIA WAS somewhat dismayed that, as soon as she set foot in the conference room, her gaze went to Justin in spite of the other people present. She barely saw Meg point out the seat she'd saved or noted that the side table actually held herbal tea today. Normally, there was just coffee, another one of Olivia's nonvices.

Instead of paying attention to any of that, her eyes followed Justin. It was as if the meeting were being captioned in the same romanticized style as their upscale catalog. *Although casually attired in dark denim and a white button-down shirt, there was nothing casual about the intimacy of his warm smile.*

She blinked. Good thing she had that vacation coming up.

Standing at the head of the table, wearing a tie that made one wonder how he'd landed a job in the fashion world, Steve Reynolds smiled. "Liv, you're here. Great, we can get started."

As someone who had spent the fourth grade as "Big Liv," she despised the nickname Liv, but not enough to remind her promotion-wielding—or withholding—boss.

People began taking seats around the dark oval table, and Steve pointed toward the still-standing Justin. "Everyone, this is Justin Hawthorne, the newest member of our team. We were lucky enough to steal him from Hilliard. Liv, he'll be your photographer for the swimsuit spread. Justin Hawthorne, meet Olivia Lockhart."

Olivia opened her mouth to tell Steve that she'd met the photographer, but Justin cut her off.

"Nice to officially make your acquaintance." He took her hand and she almost jumped, surprised by the contact and by how immediately his skin warmed hers.

He pulled his fingers away, but the heat of his touch remained. Her pulse quickened, and Olivia sat down, harboring high hopes for the calming effects of the chamomile tea Meg pushed toward her.

Steve began the meeting with his customary call for new ideas, which he preempted with his own. To his credit, Steve often had wonderful ideas, but was it really necessary to pause at studied intervals so his underlings could fawn over his brilliance? Olivia had learned that the best way to get along with her boss was to tune him out the majority of the time. Listening with half an ear for anything that might apply to her, she let her attention wander.

Unfortunately, it wandered to Justin Hawthorne two chairs down, to his smile and the brush of his hand against hers. She tried to recall what he'd smelled like, but she'd been so overwhelmed by his touch that she hadn't had time to notice. Expensive cologne? A simple aftershave? Soap?

His grin was killer, and she tried to imagine his laugh. Deep, probably. A sexy rumble of amusement. She sighed. Didn't she ever learn? When a man looked like sin in jeans, it was best to stay far away from him, not dwell on his mouth, or the color of his eyes, which were the green of very deep water off Florida's Emerald Coast....

Okay, she was fine now. She just needed to concentrate on something patently unsexy to combat Justin's appeal and the boredom of this meeting. *Aha!* Her clogged sink, filled with brown gunk that morning because something had come up through the pipes and the super hadn't come in to fix it before she left for work. Problem solved.

"...with Justin and Olivia."

At the sound of her name, Olivia's gaze shot to her boss.

"The two of you can discuss concepts and location on the drive up."

She and Justin would be riding together, staying at the same hotel. In two very separate rooms, she reminded herself, annoyed by her juvenile twinge of excitement. Plus, the models and crew would be there. Nothing cozy about the setting at all.

"Liv, I liked your preliminary layout descriptions. Just make sure you and Justin are on the same page and that we get what we need."

She had great ideas she couldn't wait to use for promoting their new line of swimwear. Of course, none of those ideas came to mind just now. She was sidetracked by images of her and her photographer, alone on a romantic beach. What was that old movie where the couple kissed as waves crashed over them?

Telling herself sand was more gritty than sexy, Olivia dutifully fixated on her broken sink. A new picture flashed behind her eyes: Justin standing in her kitchen, clothed only in a pair of jeans and a toolbelt.

Then Steve mentioned that the South Carolina trip had been moved to Thursday, and she completely— well, partially, anyway—forgot about a shirtless Justin in her apartment.

"Moved to Thursday?" She couldn't finish the two-day shoot in time to catch her Friday flight. "No one mentioned that to me."

"It was just decided," Steve explained impatiently. "Justin can't go Wednesday."

"B-but I leave for my vacation Friday." It wasn't as though flights to the small island left Hartsfield every day; who knew when she could arrange the next one? With the fashion show coming up, she'd been lucky to squeeze in time off now.

Steve shrugged. "So you'll take your vacation some other time. I know it can be rescheduled because you've already done it for us once. And we appreciate what a team player you are, Liv."

The veiled threat didn't escape her. Team players got promoted. People who balked at rescheduling got passed over and were forever doomed to small offices with no windows.

When the interminable meeting finally ended, Olivia and her co-workers slunk from the room to return to their offices and rediscover their wills to live. She had just made it inside her own office when Justin surprised her, asking from her doorway, "Are they always like that?"

"Long and boring? Yep. Steve is—" Mentally, she clapped a hand over her mouth.

Complaining with Meg at lunch away from the office was one thing. Saying something derogatory about management here, in front of someone she didn't even know, was stupid. Normally, she didn't make workplace faux pas, but she'd been distracted all day.

The reason for her distraction stepped inside, shutting the door behind him. When he bypassed the two upholstered chairs available in favor of leaning casually on the corner of her desk, she discovered that he smelled like a maddening mixture of denim, spicy cologne and male.

"I wanted to apologize for the trip postponement," he said. "Steve assured me that bending the schedule would be no problem. I never would have asked if it weren't important, but my—"

"Don't worry about it. It's fine." If her appendix burst Wednesday, Steve would have insisted she be a team player, crawl out of her hospital bed, and get her butt to South Carolina.

"Maybe I could make it up to you sometime," he suggested with a flirtatious smile. "Buy you lunch, or something."

"No!" Go out alone with Justin? Bad idea. And she didn't even want to think about the "or something." "That's not necessary."

He blinked, and she realized her immediate refusal had probably made her sound like the office poster child for PMS.

She backtracked quickly, not taking the time to organize her thoughts. "I meant to say, no, thank you. Nice offer, but, I, um, have these restrictions. Salad only." Which he most definitely *wasn't*.

"I hear a lot of places serve that now." His lazy grin held just the right amount of amusement—teasing, but not mocking.

"Right. Of course. Bad example. It's hard to explain, but I've sort of given up..." She stopped, thank God, just shy of explaining about walking chocolate. Which he most definitely *was*. "It's a diet thing."

Justin pushed himself away from the desk, shaking his head. "Don't tell me you're one of those women."

"Excuse me?" Unless he meant one of those women who couldn't string together a coherent sentence— which she blamed on how good he smelled—he was about to be in trouble.

"Someone with hang-ups about her body, who always wishes she were skinnier."

The angry heat that blazed through her had nothing to do with his hitting close to home, it was based on principle. "You've known me for a matter of *hours*, Mr. Hawthorne, and you think that gives you the right to diagnose any so-called hang-ups?"

He grimaced. "In my defense, I was headed toward a compliment."

"Yeah?" She crossed her arms. "Well, you took a wrong turn somewhere."

His gaze slid down her body. "What I should have said is that you...don't need to..."

He trailed off, his male admiration too frank to need words. Olivia tried to be offended by the perusal— who the hell was he to so boldly assess her and pronounce judgment? Her body, on the other hand, must've missed the memo on political correctness. Her skin prickled with awareness, growing warmer. His expression shifted as he raised his eyes back to hers. The appreciation had been replaced by something deeper, more urgent, and Olivia swallowed.

Even if she'd been able to muster any indignation, it would have been a tad hypocritical coming from someone so recently having toolbelt fantasies.

"Justin, I—"

"That's an improvement," he interrupted approvingly. "Much better than 'Mr. Hawthorne.' I'd like us to be on a friendly basis."

Just how friendly did he have in mind? Desire swirled through her abdomen, warm and thick and slow, like honey.

"Olivia?" A knock accompanied Jeanie's voice on the other side of the closed door.

Blinking, Olivia tried to reorient herself to her surroundings. For a moment there, she'd forgotten she was even at the office. Carefully looking past Justin, not wanting to risk meeting his eyes again, she called back, "Come on in, Jeanie. I have those proofs ready."

The door opened and Jeanie stepped inside, her expression hesitant. "I didn't mean to interrupt. I—hello. You must be Justin."

Smiling, he shook Jeanie's hand, and annoyance caught Olivia off guard. A moment ago, he'd used that smile on her. Had she reacted with the same girlish, awestruck expression that was now on Jeanie's face? Probably. Less than a full day into a new resolution to change her dating diet, and here she'd been, devouring Justin with her eyes and going all trembly and fluttery inside when he locked gazes with her.

She just needed some distance, time to regroup and strengthen her resolve.

Once Jeanie had the manila folder she'd come in for, she walked away, stopping at the door with an inquisitive glance in Olivia's direction.

"Please, leave it open," Olivia said. "Justin was on his way out."

Judging from his raised eyebrows, this was news to him, but he turned without argument. As Jeanie had done, he paused at the entrance to the office. "We can just finish our discussion later," he said with a wink.

He'd winked at her? It was such a kitschy thing to do, yet she didn't hear bad '70s pickup lines in her head. Instead, she was tempted to smile. The only thing that kept her from doing so was the threat of "finishing" their chat. Let's see, which part was she most eager to revisit—why she didn't think it would be a good idea to have lunch with him, what he thought of her figure, or how attuned their bodies had been? *No thank you.* With any luck, this little encounter would never come up again.

As if she'd ever had any luck with men.

AFTER A NIGHT spent in an apartment empty of her exboyfriend's presence and her ex-roommate's couch, Olivia entered the office Tuesday with renewed resolve. Her thoughts had strayed to Justin Hawthorne several times during the night, but echoes of heartache and humiliation had quelled her unwise attraction. Lifting her chin, Olivia strode toward her office, saying good morning to Jeanie as she passed. *I'm here to work, not think about men.*

Three hours later, she leaned back in her chair, congratulating herself on a productive morning. She'd even managed a quick conversation with Steve on the interoffice line without wanting to strangle the man with his own necktie.

"I deserve a break," she muttered, stretching her muscles as she stood. A cup of tea sounded good, and maybe she'd drop by Meg's office on the way back from the break room, see if her friend had any fun model gossip this morning.

The break room was a beige room with scuffed cabinets and absolutely zero decorative qualities. There was, however, always a ready supply of hot and cold beverages, the day's copy of the *Atlanta Journal-Constitution* to read, and usually people with whom to shoot the breeze. All in all, a good source of procrastination.

Today, the coffee room's inhabitants were female, with one notable exception.

Justin Hawthorne sat in a blue plastic chair amid five women, including Kate from HR; Steve's personal secretary, Diane; a couple of ladies from accounting; and even sixty-seven-year-old Ms. Phipps, who kept casting wish-I-were-forty-years-younger glances in Justin's direction.

The admiring glances Olivia could empathize with, but really, had Diane forgotten this was a place of business? When the curvy redhead asked Justin if she could have the issue of the *AJC* lying on the table in front of him, she managed to phrase the request in a breathless sultry tone that insinuated she wanted something much more. Instead of waiting for him to hand her the paper, she slowly leaned forward, brushing against him in a way Kate could have used as the what-not-to-do example in her sexual-harassment seminar.

Waggling his eyebrows, Justin said something in a low voice that caused Diane to laugh, and Olivia ground her teeth. Her annoyance was only heightened when she couldn't help an admiring glance of her own. No man should look that good! His all-black attire today was a great foil for his light hair and bright eyes.

Basic black is back, and what could be sexier?

The man lounged in his chair like a sexy monarch surveying his coffee-scented kingdom. Or a sheikh with his harem. Olivia reached blankly for one of the mugs kept over the sink, but instead of seeing the cabinet in front of her, she envisioned herself in a flimsy costume of veils, summoned by Justin to—

"Morning." His warm deep voice in her ear caused her to jump, and she clenched the handle of the blue mug to keep from dropping it.

"Justin! I didn't notice you." More accurately, she'd been too lost in her own torrid fantasies to see him stand up.

"Apparently." He raised a dark blond brow. "Not very flattering, you realize."

Olivia said nothing as she filled her mug with water. Was his teasing comment an invitation for her to appease his ego? Why would he need it when, as far as she could tell, the other women in the room had been generously feeding his self-esteem?

Sean's parting words echoed in her mind. *It wouldn't be fair to the women of the world to limit myself to just one.*

Was Justin cut from the same cloth? Wanting that sixth woman's attention when he already had the adoration of five, including a gorgeous redheaded secretary who was now glaring daggers at Olivia? Was that all the moment of sexual connection in her office yesterday had been about? For a few seconds, with his eyes on hers, he'd made her feel no one existed beyond the two of them, but maybe he would have behaved the same with any other woman.

Justin reached past Olivia to the coffeemaker, glancing over his shoulder at the female-inhabited table. "Did you want sugar in this, Ms. Phipps?"

"Two packets, please."

As he stirred the sugar into the cup he'd just filled, Olivia sighed. It was much easier to maintain her cynical image of the man when he was enjoying Diane's cleavage instead of doing a favor for the elderly Ms. Phipps.

Diane, however, wasn't impressed with his small act of kindness. She left the room in an I'm-not-used-to-sharing-a-man's-attention huff. The two women Olivia recognized from accounting followed behind, chatting as they walked, but they both shot wistful glances in Justin's direction.

Seemingly oblivious, he handed Ms. Phipps her cup of coffee.

The older woman smiled. "Thank you, but I should be getting back to work now, too."

"My loss," Justin said with a rakish smile.

Olivia grabbed a single-serving bag of decaffeinated tea, wondering if he was a great guy who was kind to his elders, or if he was just so in the habit of flirting that he never turned it off.

After the small exodus of women, the only one remaining was Kate, who sidled closer to Justin and delicately cleared her throat. "So, um, about that dinner...."

"I'll call you after the South Carolina trip," Justin said. "You pick out the restaurant."

Not a week on the job and he already had a date. *Now why isn't that surprising?* The only surprise was that his plans were with fresh-faced Kate and not Diane, who stood a better chance at holding her own with a man in Justin's league. Trying to look like something other than a disapproving eavesdropper, Olivia set her mug in the microwave.

Kate bounced out of the room with the enthusiasm of a teenager who'd just been asked to the prom, and Olivia almost winced on the poor girl's behalf. When Olivia had been younger, she'd worn her heart on her sleeve in much the same way...but after it had been broken a few times, she'd moved it for safekeeping.

Instead of also leaving now that his admirers had gone, Justin leaned against the counter. She watched the microwave, willing it to beep. Thursday, when she'd be trapped in the car with him, was plenty soon enough to be alone with him. She pondered the possibility of his becoming less sexy between now and then. Was there a polite, logical way to insist he didn't wear black?

Probably not.

TRYING NOT TO BE too obvious, Justin studied his beautiful co-worker. Her gray eyes were frosty today, with no hint of the molten silver desire he'd seen—and felt—yesterday in her office. He wanted to cajole her into a more receptive mood, to prove the woman he'd seen glimpses of was in there somewhere.

"How's your day going, Liv?" He assumed she went by the office nickname, but, personally, he didn't think it suited her.

The more lyrical *Olivia* fit perfectly—as did the navy turtleneck and long tailored skirt she wore. There was a sexy contrast between how little skin was revealed and how boldly the lush curves of her body were delineated. Stopping short of a noticeable leer, he discreetly traced those curves with his gaze, wishing it were with his hands instead.

"Fine." She dipped her tea bag in her mug. "Busy."

Not a woman of many words.

Licking her lips, she took a step forward to go around him. "I should be getting back to my office."

The scent of her light floral perfume and the warmer fragrance of her body wafted over him. "You smell incredible."

She froze, spine rigid, her only movement the now double-time dunking of her tea. If he didn't know better, he'd say her expression was hurt. He was willing to admit that yesterday, when he'd commented on her figure, his words had come out wrong, but now he could only conclude that the lady didn't take flattery well. She ducked her head, and her long wavy hair fell over her shoulder in a dark curtain, partially obscuring her face.

"I meant it in the complimentary sense," he said.

"Yes. I know."

"I thought women liked it when men notice personal details and comment."

"Maybe some do." She looked up then, her eyes steely. "Personally, I've had my fill of handsome charmers with ulterior motives."

"Now hold on a second." Noticing the way her skirt hugged her tight perfect derriere wasn't a *motive.* He'd get back to that handsome and charming part later. "I—"

"I apologize." She exhaled, her shoulders rounding. "You said something kind, and I was rude."

More defensive than rude, and her eyes reflected a vulnerability that seemed an odd reaction to a comment on her perfume.

Justin told himself to end this exchange and forget it ever happened. After the responsibilities of the last few years, responsibilities that unofficially ended tomorrow night, he'd earned the right to uncomplicated fun. Olivia's changing moods and mixed signals screamed complications.

A man with any brains would ask Diane out when he got back from South Carolina. He'd been caught off guard by Kate's dinner invitation and reflexively said yes, but she seemed like a sweet kid who needed an equally sweet boyfriend. Justin was looking for something a little less lasting—simple, clear-cut, adult enjoyment.

He looked into Olivia's soft gray eyes, and desire tightened his body. Too bad he didn't think the offer of no-strings fun would appeal to her.

"Maybe I should be the one apologizing," he said, "if my remarks were too personal for the workplace."

"No, I overreacted. I've been...never mind. Maybe you really are a nice guy."

"Just 'maybe'?" he teased, giving her a look of mock-indignation.

She laughed, and the husky sound affected him even more viscerally than when he'd overheard it yesterday, because this time he'd won it from her. Her open, welcoming expression was unexpected and transformed her from attractive to so sexy his breath caught.

He held the door open, and as she passed by, she tossed one last smile over her shoulder. "I really am sorry if I've been curt. I'm glad we're going to be working together, Justin."

So was he. Particularly if he got to work with *this* Olivia, not the one behind the guarded mask. He'd just have to see what he could do to keep this Olivia around more often.

3

WEDNESDAY EVENING, long after the daily noise of the office had dropped to just a few remaining employees shutting down their computers, Jeanie poked her head through the doorway to Olivia's office. "I'm about to take off."

Olivia waggled her fingers in a half wave. "See you tomorrow." Unfortunately. No sunny Kaokara for her.

The blonde hovered indecisively, fidgeting until Olivia finally asked, "Something else I can do for you?"

"Are you sure you don't want to come to dinner with us? Albert's brother is very nice."

"Thanks anyway, but I'm just going to head home."

Having made one last failed effort at the double date, Jeanie nodded. The other woman was gone before Olivia could admit anything stupid—such as, she'd be a lousy dinner date with Justin Hawthorne on her mind.

Could he really be the exception womankind hoped for, the stunningly sexy man who was still a nice guy? After their brief interlude in the breakroom yesterday, she'd chided herself for having painted him with the same brush as Sean just because he was good-looking. So he and Kate were having dinner sometime after the shoot, that was hardly grounds for labeling him Womanizer of the Year.

Her stomach growled, turning her thoughts from Justin's future dinner plans to her own immediate ones. She gathered her belongings and took the elevator down to her car, looking forward to food and a relaxing bath. About halfway to her apartment, however, she realized that she'd finished off her emergency store of groceries the night before. The sole contents of her fridge were wilted lettuce and half-empty condiment bottles of everything from lime juice to Worcestershire sauce.

Deli takeout it is, then.

By the time she pulled into a parking garage close to her favorite downtown delicatessen, she was starving. She hurried across the sidewalk, her trench coat not completely protecting her from the crisp evening air. As she waited at the intersection for oncoming traffic to stop, she shot an envious sidelong glance toward the expensive four-star restaurant on the corner.

Lacking an occasion big enough to justify the price tag, she'd never dined there. Now, she unconsciously pressed a hand to her empty stomach and fantasized about the meals lucky patrons were enjoying inside. She covertly studied the candlelit booths on the other side of the thick glass window and tried not to feel too much like a gastronomical Peeping Tom.

Justin.

Her jaw dropped as she did a double take. Yes, that was definitely Justin Hawthorne inside.

Aware she was staring openly, Olivia snapped her gaze to the blinking red upraised hand across the street. But a quick glance back showed Justin hadn't noticed her. His attention was fully devoted to the beautiful blonde seated across from him, a slim young woman in a little black dress.

The blonde reached across the table for Justin's hand, and anger churned in the pit of Olivia's stomach. She'd rescheduled her vacation for a dinner date! She should be in South Carolina tonight and en route to her vacation Friday, but Justin had ruined that with his "emergency."

The sign on the other side of the crosswalk finally changed, flashing the picture of a stick-figure pedestrian, and she marched forward, fuming. She wasn't an unreasonable woman. If tonight's date had been, for instance, an anniversary or a marriage proposal, she could've understood. But if the blonde was a serious girlfriend, what was he doing flirting with Diane and making dinner plans with Kate?

Either leading on the poor sweet kid from HR, or taking a leaf from Sean's book and cheating on his girlfriend.

Fists clenched, Olivia entered the deli. As the warm air and aroma of fresh-baked bread hit her, she realized she didn't actually have much of an appetite left. She'd spent all day castigating herself for hastily judging him, telling herself that his being attractive wasn't a crime. She'd apologized to him, made a point of being extra friendly when she'd seen him in the parking garage this morning—only to learn he was like too many other men, interested in beautiful women and his own selfish pleasure. Forget work or any inconvenience to anyone else's life.

Her first self-protective instincts about Justin Hawthorne had been right. Every inch The Guy, a creature with more testosterone than conscience, he should have a bright orange warning label smacked across his forehead. Why couldn't she learn once and for all to stop pushing aside prudence in favor of a handsome smile?

JUSTIN WALKED into the dim smoky interior of Hewitt's Bar shortly before midnight. Although he'd need to get out of bed before dawn to drive Andrea to the airport, he'd been restless after they'd returned from dinner, so he'd called his friend Bryan Tanner to meet for a couple of beers and a game of pool. On the weekend, when management brought a DJ in, Hewitt's was a popular spot to socialize and meet women. In the middle of the week, business was slightly slower, and it was a great place to come for a quick drink.

Lifting his gaze to the television set above the bar that was broadcasting the day's sports highlights, Justin waited for his chance to order. He'd drink to getting his life back. Tomorrow, his nineteen-year-old-sister Andrea would leave for a prestigious cooking school in Europe. His obligation would be fulfilled.

When his parents had been killed in a boating accident shortly after his twenty-second birthday, Justin had taken on the unexpected responsibility of raising his two sisters. A decade older than Andrea, with Lisa in the middle, he'd made a lot of unplanned changes to his young bachelor life to set a good example and supplement the life insurance settlement to provide for his sisters. He loved them both dearly, but over the years, whenever the situation had been especially stressful, he'd repeatedly vowed that as soon as he had the house to himself, he would make up for lost time.

That started tomorrow. Lisa was in a co-op program at Auburn, with a job lined up after next year's graduation, and now Andy was headed abroad.

A woman shuffling a round plastic tray jostled him. "Hey, handsome. Don't usually see you in here so late."

He smiled at the blond waitress—Natalie, if he recalled correctly. "I had something to celebrate."

"You'll be here all night if you wait on Kurt." She nodded to the other side of the room where the bartender was taking his time mixing a drink for an attractive patron. "Have a seat in my section, and I'll bring something over."

Justin asked for a draft beer, then chose an empty booth against the wall. His future loomed promising and new, devoid of helping anyone with homework, having awkward discussions about dating or attending sports events and milestone ceremonies that their parents should have been here to see.

Natalie sauntered up to his table with a full frosty mug. "So what are we celebrating?"

The freedom to walk around at home stark naked if he felt like it, the freedom not to worry that he was a lousy day-to-day role model. "New job."

Freelance photography hadn't been dependable enough for a man raising two sisters and the travel that had excited him became an obstacle. He'd taken a job in design at Hilliard, but had jumped at the chance to join Sweet Nothings now that they were expanding.

On-staff photographers were costly, and Justin, though his portfolio displayed his talent, lacked the experience other candidates could have used to negotiate more money.

"Good for you," Natalie congratulated him. "Drink's on the house, then."

"You don't have to do that," he said, knowing "on the house" probably meant out of her pocket.

"Honey, you'd be surprised what I pull down in tips. I don't know if you've noticed, but I'm a good-looking woman," she said with a grin.

"Trust me, I noticed. I'm guessing your boss would object to your sharing a drink with me right now... maybe another time?"

"Ah, but see, *that* my boyfriend would object to."

"Boyfriend, huh?" He lifted the mug. "Then I'm no longer celebrating. I'm officially drowning my sorrows."

She laughed. "Beer's nice and multipurpose that way. Don't worry, a guy who looks like you won't be lonely long. You never know," she added before moving toward the next table, "maybe you'll meet someone at this new job."

Olivia Lockhart's face came to mind, but he banished it immediately. *Never gonna happen.* Despite finding their way to friendlier ground in the breakroom yesterday and chatting amiably in the parking garage this morning, he still couldn't imagine Olivia agreeing to meet him for drinks. She'd find a polite way to turn him down, then avoid him around the office.

"Hey, buddy." Bryan Tanner, rumpled and grinning

as ever, slid in on the other side of the booth, making quick eye contact with Natalie as she passed.

Justin nodded in greeting. "What's with the lumberjack look?"

His dark-haired friend didn't truly look like a lumberjack, but the flannel shirt and unshaven stubble along his jaw invited taunting. Heckling each other unofficially cemented their friendship, and since Bryan so often won by default of actually having a life, Justin took his shots where he could get them.

"Go ahead, make fun if you want," Bryan said with a sly smile, "but the ladies love the casual look."

The ladies obviously loved *something* because Justin's friend never hurt for dates.

Bryan did lucrative contract work setting up network systems all over the country, but between jobs, he roosted in Atlanta. While Justin would never come out and say anything so touchy-feely, he was grateful for the way his friend had stayed in contact despite the traveling. Other ex-college buddies had drifted off sooner, unable to relate to Justin's sudden domestic crises and raising two young women in the suburbs. Watching Bryan bounce around from place to place, coming home to a different woman each visit, Justin had often envied his friend's life.

"I don't get it." Justin shook his head. "You're a glorified computer nerd. Do you *pay* women to spend time with you, or are they compelled by pity?"

Bryan grinned. "It's all that talk about my hardware. Master and slave drives are nice openers, too."

Natalie edged up to the table with a bottle of Bryan's regular beer.

"Thank you, sweet thing. Tell me you aren't still seeing that boyfriend of yours."

"Afraid I am." Natalie smiled at her favorite customer. "And he could still kick your ass, in case that was your next question."

Justin laughed. "Oh, yeah, that's quite the way with women you have, Bry."

"I can't believe I'm getting flack from you," Bryan complained as the waitress moved away. "The Dateless Wonder."

An exaggeration, but one with more truth than he would have liked. "Dateless no more. As of tomorrow, you are looking at a man free to accept room keys from hot models."

"Well, hell, I'll drink to that."

Since Justin had done everything possible to make sure his sisters didn't discover sex until their twenties—or preferably, never—it had seemed wrong to spend his nights elsewhere or to sneak women into the house. There had been one or two relationships, of course, and the occasional weekend when both his sisters were gone, but overall, his love life had not been the stuff a man in his twenties dreams about.

Now, with thirty looming at the end of the month, he had definite plans to make the most of his bachelorhood. He needed some time to focus on himself and not be responsible to or for anyone. He could make dinner plans with a woman without checking the family calendar to see if he was obligated to be anywhere, he could have women over any night of the week.

"So, you gonna introduce me to some of these hot models?" Bryan asked.

"Not a chance," Justin said with a laugh. "In case there *is* a woman in the 404 area code you haven't dated yet, I'd like to meet her first."

Sweet Nothings was his opportunity for a fresh start. At Hilliard, he'd been the guy who'd missed work when Lisa had her wisdom teeth pulled, the guy who'd taken Andy to the office Christmas party when her loser boyfriend dumped her right at the holidays. But now he was simply Justin Hawthorne, single photographer.

Bryan stood. "C'mon, you said something about a pool game. Try not to cry like a little girl when I take your money."

"Give it your best shot. I'll even let you break, but I gotta warn you, I'm feeling pretty lucky."

Andrea and Lisa were both happy and succeeding on their chosen paths, he loved his new job, and he'd reached a good understanding with Olivia yesterday. Even if she wasn't interested in celebrating his new-found freedom with him, that didn't mean he couldn't make the most out of working side by side with her. And there were plenty of other mermaids in the sea.

Tomorrow he left for a beach shoot with lingerie models. How much better did one guy's life get?

No complications, he promised himself.

JEANIE STOOD in Olivia's office early Thursday morning, theoretically helping with a last-minute check to make sure Olivia wasn't forgetting anything. In reality, she was mooning over Justin, who had peeked his head in a second ago to tell Olivia he was ready when she was.

"Isn't he delicious?" The receptionist sighed. "The man is practically edible."

Olivia wouldn't mind Justin at her dinner table—with his head on a platter.

"I bumped into him outside Steve's office this morning," Jeanie confided, "and, for a second, I thought he was flirting with me. Much nicer pick-me-up than coffee!"

He probably *had* been flirting with her. The skunk. "I thought you were in love with Albert."

"I am. But even I have to admit, he's no Justin."

Exactly! The Justins of the world were the sexy men women sighed over...and later cried over. The Alberts of the world were the reliable ones who paid bills on time and never cheated on their wives. Once her promotion was in the bag, Olivia would find herself a nice solid Albert.

Last night, she'd gone home to torture herself with the image of Justin in that restaurant with the blonde. She'd also entertained fantasies of confronting him, but that would be like yelling at a leopard about its spots. Pointless.

Though she was entitled to her righteous indignation, fighting with Justin would only be counterproductive. Those up for promotion practiced good people skills and didn't antagonize Steve's newest office favorite. Besides, she and Justin needed to cooperate to have a decent shoot. She was adult enough to work with the man and ignore his tawdry personal life.

The receptionist zipped up the laptop in its black carry bag. "Think you're all set, Liv."

Olivia bit down on her tongue. It wasn't the younger woman's fault that the nickname had spread.

"Your cell phone is charged," Jeanie continued, "and that's all the files you asked for. Justin has the keys to the company car, and I had one of the guys transfer your suitcase to the trunk."

"Thanks, Jeanie." Olivia picked up her coat and folded it over her arm. "Have a great weekend."

Reaching the elevator just as the doors were closing, she quickened her steps. "Wait! Hold the elevator, please."

The silver doors slid back, revealing Justin Hawthorne, an appealing masculine picture in his leather bomber jacket and well-fitting khaki slacks.

"Hey." He grinned. "I was going to get the map out of my car, then come back upstairs and chauvinistically harass you about how long it takes women to get ready."

Her jaw tightened. No doubt he thought his teasing was cute.

At her pinched expression, Justin reached out and touched her shoulder. "You feeling all right this morning?"

The cotton that separated his hand from her bare flesh seemed to enhance his touch rather than protect her from it. "Fine. Thank you." Why didn't knowing what kind of man he was stop the zing that zipped through her?

It was just the elevator, she assured herself as she scooted slightly out of reach. The enclosed space forced her to stand so close she could feel the warmth of his body and breathe in his unique personal scent, which she already knew too well. Steamy scenes from different movies flashed through her mind, and she wondered why she'd never noticed how sensual elevators were before.

Stop it. You've learned from your mistakes, remember? Fantasizing about sex with Justin against the elevator wall was not the sign of a wiser woman. If nothing else, the blinking red light of the security camera mounted in the corner brought her back to reality.

The elevator wobbled slightly as it finished its descent, and the doors parted. Olivia stepped forward purposefully. Justin followed, lifting a key ring and unlocking the company car with an audible beep.

Hours together loomed ahead, but she could handle the ride. Speak to him only when necessary and ignore him the rest of the time.

Whenever that got difficult, she'd remind herself of how he'd smiled and complimented her in the break room the other day and how, for a brief moment, she'd been foolish enough to imagine a real connection between them.

4

SINCE MICROMANAGING was not part of her leadership style, Olivia stood to the side, shoes kicked off, the sand cool and smooth beneath her bare feet. Though intermittently windy, especially here by the water, it was a beautiful day—unseasonably warm, if still a little chilly for the bathing suits they were photographing. Squinting against the sand-flecked breeze, Justin took the white diffusion dome from an assistant and measured the light with a handheld flashmeter.

Olivia's personal feelings about him notwithstanding, he'd been doing a great job. She watched him adjust an aluminum reflector to modify the way sunlight fell across Stormy.

While none of Sweet Nothings' models was a famous Frederique or Tyra, several of them were becoming increasingly well known, and the hotel staff was excited to be hosting such a glamorous endeavor on its private stretch of beach. Like their bigger competitors, such as the notable Victoria's Secret, Sweet Nothings was taking what it knew about push-up bras and tummy-flattering panels and applying it to sexy swimwear.

Stormy and Felicia posed in daring suits while everyone else wore clothes more appropriate to the early-spring weather. Resplendent in a bright red string bikini, Stormy was blond with eyes that actually were the gray-violet of storm clouds, thanks to the modern miracle of colored contacts. Chestnut-haired, green-eyed Felicia wore a blue one-piece with so many cutouts and straps that she managed to reveal as much flesh as her counterpart. Both women were perfectly, if artificially, tanned.

The sirens of old lured men with their songs, but you won't need to sing a note to catch his attention while wearing one of our signature bathing suits.

Unable to shake her copywriting roots, Olivia dreamed up ad passages while Justin took picture after picture, first with a digital camera, then a traditional one. She couldn't help noticing that Felicia put a little extra something into her smiles. And why not? Justin had been openly admiring her since the shoot had begun.

I don't care that he flirts with models.

But indifference shouldn't burn and stick in her throat. When Justin stopped to reload film and the models stepped behind the portable changing screens to don the next preselected suits, Olivia stole a moment for herself, strolling away a few feet. She inhaled deeply, breathing in the salty musk of sea and sand, hoping to dispel her fixation with the photographer who was as adept at charming women as he was at snapping pictures.

THOUGH Justin was looking through the viewfinder of his camera, he knew the moment Olivia started across the beach. His involuntary awareness of the woman was unshakable.

In the car, she'd been almost stiffly businesslike. He'd tried not to let this newest shift bother him. Today *was* about business. But after they'd arrived here, and he'd seen how friendly she was with others...

Earlier, Justin had been both distracted and annoyed by Olivia laughing with Rick, a makeup artist who freely admitted he'd gone into this line of business to be around beautiful women. Olivia certainly qualified. Probably in deference to the wind, she'd pulled her hair up today, somehow containing all of it in one of those toothy plastic clips that defy the laws of physics. The feminine curve of her neck and elegant features of her face were impossible to miss. Justin could no more ignore her than he could understand why *he* was the only one on the receiving end of her all-work-no-play demeanor.

So many things about Olivia contradicted each other—her confident professionalism and the occasional vulnerability he thought he glimpsed in her gaze, the moments of awareness that had simmered between them, only to be replaced by aloofness, the way she kidded with those on her crew but kept her responses to Justin on a speak-when-spoken-to basis.

Maybe his perverse preoccupation with her was just a determination to solve the mystery of her behavior, but he couldn't resist reeling her back in as she wandered toward the water. "How much more do you want out here?"

They'd discussed in the car that he should also take some shots at the hotel's heated indoor pool where the lighting was easier to control and the water warmed.

Olivia walked back toward him while the models had their makeup retouched. "We should get as much as we can this afternoon. Rick said there's a cold front moving in tonight, which makes tomorrow perfect for the inside stuff."

Once again, though there was nothing openly antagonistic in her words or expression, she seemed to stare through him more than see him. A frustration Justin didn't normally encounter with the opposite sex filled him. He was self-aware enough to know most women found him attractive. There had even been moments when he would have sworn Olivia did.

But what did he know? Because he'd also believed they'd reached a turning point in their working relationship, and today had dispelled that myth.

Now wasn't the time to pursue the issue, though. Felicia and Stormy headed down the beach, ready for the single round of shots that would take place in the water.

"Gorgeous," he told Felicia as she frolicked in knee-deep surf. "Men will hyperventilate when they see this."

"They'd better." She pursed her lush lips in a mock pout. "This water is freezing."

He recalled how closely Olivia had been standing earlier to Rick of the bleached white teeth. Why had Justin been paying attention to that instead of focusing more on the invitation in Felicia's smiles? The model was playful and flirtatious, the type who would enjoy herself during a fling but not take it too seriously afterward.

"Don't worry," he promised her. "I'll get you warmed up as soon as this is over."

Her meadow-green eyes widened. "I'll hold you to that."

"What about me?" Stormy demanded, throwing her head back and pausing as he snapped a picture. "I'm cold, too."

"No guy with working eyesight could forget you," he said. "And don't worry I've got plenty of...coffee and blankets to go around."

Stormy laughed. Not to be ignored, Felicia upped her vamping for the camera. Damn, but he was getting some great shots. The next two hours flew by, and Justin's love of photography temporarily eclipsed his tension.

As soon as they were finished and he was packing up his cameras, however, Olivia rushed back to the forefront of his mind. Though she was discussing something with one of the crew, her gunmetal-gray eyes were zeroed in on Justin, the disapproval in them canceling out the warmth of the afternoon sun.

Now what?

He'd been flirting, but it hadn't been with her, so she couldn't object this time. If Stormy and Felicia weren't complaining, where was the problem? The results, caught on film, would benefit everyone at Sweet Nothings.

"We got some great work done today," Olivia told the assembled group. "Enjoy your evening, but remember we have an early start, so don't make it a late night."

Was he getting paranoid, or did she aim that at him?

He stalked toward her, wanting answers. "May I talk to you?"

"Um, sure. Just not now. I'm feeling kind of gritty and want to get cleaned up. We've got a private dinner buffet in one of the dining rooms. Talk there?"

Before he could answer—hell, before she'd even finished her question—she pivoted on her heel and headed toward the hotel. The feeling that he'd been summarily dismissed grated on the one nerve he had left regarding that woman.

"Nice shoot." Felicia sidled up to him, wrapped in an oversize towel. "You're good."

He managed to subdue his anger with Olivia long enough to respond. "Thanks, but my job's easy when I have models like you and Stormy to work with."

She inclined her head in gracious acknowledgment of the praise. "Any plans after dinner? I was thinking about checking out that indoor pool area before tomorrow. You know, like research. I understand there's a hot tub. And you did offer to make sure I got warm again."

"I—" Realizing that his bad mood had almost led to passing up hot-tubbing with a lingerie model, he mentally kicked himself. Was he insane? "Sure. Hitting the hot tub sounds great." Yet not as great as it should.

Olivia's fault. She had him so ticked off that he couldn't fully enjoy what any man in his right mind would recognize as paradise. Which just ticked him off even more.

She might have postponed their conversation, but he and Olivia Lockhart were going to get this settled. Very soon.

OLIVIA LEFT the dining room, the soles of her canvas shoes thudding against the lobby's marble floor as she tried to ignore her sense of guilt. Maybe it was just her dark sweater and jeans that made her feel like a thief sneaking away in the night. She'd come down for a quick bite to eat, and having accomplished that, she was now returning to her room—without having that discussion Justin had wanted. Was it her fault if he'd been too busy talking to Stormy to notice Olivia?

Okay, so she'd slunk into the room after she'd known everyone else would already be there and had only stayed long enough to gobble down half a salad before leaving while he was still otherwise occupied, but the principle of the thing was the same. Sort of.

Stopping at the elevator bay, she pressed the up button and waited. One day down, one left, then she'd be back home, not standing on a beach forced to spend hour after hour watching her sexy photographer.

You don't think he's sexy, you think he's a jerk.

A sexy jerk.

Inside the elevator, she punched the number for the appropriate floor and rolled her eyes inwardly at the orchestral intro to a made-for-elevators remix of an old Police tune. As the doors began to slide closed, a hand shot between them, followed by an arm in a long-sleeved gray shirt she unfortunately recognized. The doors sprang back, and Justin Hawthorne entered, his expression triggering an automatic uh-oh inside her.

Blond brows scrunched together in a scowl, eyes hard as emeralds, he did not look happy.

Now that the doors were open, she glanced out in the lobby, hoping for someone else who needed to go upstairs. Luck wasn't with her, but one would think she'd be used to that.

"Wh-which floor do you need?" she asked. Darn it, she hadn't meant to sound all breathy, as though she were nervous. Or, worse, attracted to him. She stoutly refused to be either. Number fourteen was already lit, but she wished she had an excuse to hit three and leave sooner.

"I'll just ride up with you." He made it sound like a challenge. "We were supposed to have a chat, remember?"

His accusatory stance and the way he crossed his arms over his chest set her teeth on edge.

"I remember that I was supposed to be headed off on vacation tomorrow." Though she'd sworn not to broach this topic, bringing it up made her feel better, as if suddenly she could breathe more deeply. She wasn't the type to be quietly wronged.

"Vacation? Is that why you're being so uptight?"

He was criticizing *her*?

She jabbed her index finger into his chest, hating that she noticed how tightly muscled it was. "I'm sorry if you've confused my adult restraint with being uptight, but not all of us have to hit on every member of the opposite sex we encounter."

"Every member?" Green flame flared in his eyes. "When was I hitting on you? Or is that the problem— jealous, Liv?"

Men and their egos! "Try relieved. I'd hate to be like Kate or that cute little blonde at the restaurant and get suckered in by your—"

"Blonde? Restaurant?"

The words avalanched out of her, her tone growing colder with each syllable. "The ritzy one downtown, where I saw you and the blonde in the black dress on your date last night. You know, the date that was so important you inconvenienced my life without so much as a second thought. Since when is wining and dining someone—"

He pressed a finger to her lips, and Olivia gasped in surprise, startled by the heat of his skin. She felt branded.

"That blonde," he said, "was my kid sister Andrea. She's going away to school in Europe. It was her last night in the States, which I wasn't about to miss. And I *tried* to tell you about it in your office the other day, but you cut me off."

Olivia couldn't have been more uncomfortable if she'd been wearing a thong two sizes too small. She'd seen a hot guy with a pretty young woman and had taken a running leap toward the nearest conclusion without even considering other logical possibilities. Obviously previous experiences had left her jaded, but her past wasn't Justin's fault.

She'd screwed up. Royally. "Your sister?"

He'd yet to move his finger, and as she spoke, her tongue caught the tip of it, tasting his skin, warm and faintly salty. He jerked his hand back, but didn't actually step away and put the safe distance she longed for between them.

Olivia swallowed. "I, um, I owe you an apology."

His gaze captured hers, and she saw her words hadn't mollified him. His hand shot past her to the control panel and the red stop button.

"What are you doing?" She braced herself for an alarm, but when Justin pressed the button, the only sirens were in her head, blaring that being stuck here with him couldn't possibly be a good idea.

The elevator lurched to a halt, but she'd been so busy trying to steady herself mentally that she hadn't paid enough attention to her physical balance. She slid forward, her body connecting with his.

His chest and thighs were firm and unyielding. She, however, seemed to soften and sink into him. The heat from their pressed-together bodies threatened to melt something inside her. Her breasts, cushioned against him, felt even fuller, tingling, and her limbs were heavy with a sensual contentment that prohibited her from moving.

"Why did you do that?" she asked, her breathing so shallow she had trouble getting the words out. He couldn't possibly know about her earlier elevator fantasies, could he? Or that he'd featured a starring role in them?

"We're going to get past this. Right here, right now," he told her, leaving her to wonder what "this" was. "I'm new to Sweet Nothings, and I like my job. I want to do well. I don't deserve the constant antagonism."

"I said I was sorry for assuming the worst. I didn't even know you had a sister," she muttered toward his chest.

He tipped her chin up with his hand. "You were abrupt before that. Disapproving, even."

Olivia took a self-protective step backward. "I admit I made a rash assumption last night, but do you deny flirting with the models today, or with Diane or Kate?"

"Flirting, sure. Holding wild orgies, no. So lay off the condemnation. I'm a single adult, as are they, and I deserve a little time for myself."

"If I had a dollar for every time I'd heard a variation on that theme!" Heaping more "condemnation" on him probably wasn't the wisest move, but pent-up anger couldn't be turned off like a faucet. "'I'm going through a me phase.' 'It's not you, honey, it's just that I need some space.' 'I need to be selfish for a little while.'"

"Maybe if *you* took a little 'me-time' you wouldn't be so tense and bitter."

"If that's your way of insinuating that I need to get laid, you—"

"No. Just stop being so self-righteous. Don't be afraid to admit you have human urges like everyone else."

Urges that in the past had netted her nothing but pain. "Of course I do, but I also have self-control. Which is what separates me from people like you."

He drew back, his expression first surprised, then angry. But when he spoke, it was in a silken whisper that was far more sultry than enraged. "Let's just test that self-control, shall we?"

When she opened her mouth to argue, his finger returned, not to shush her this time, but to trace the shape of her lips, dipping inside her mouth once, teasingly. Her annoyance hadn't magically disappeared, exactly, but fighting had dredged her emotions to the surface—even the unwise emotions she'd been battling. Hard to say if the flush of her skin and her accelerated pulse were from anger or desire.

His eyes locked with hers as he continued the simple seduction. Kissing him would be a horrible mistake, but the powerful attraction that had been building since she'd first laid eyes on him was heightened to new levels, by his touch and intoxicating scent—and her own not-so-buried feelings about elevators. Later, she'd regret the mistake.

But that was later.

JUSTIN MOVED IN slowly, unsure whether he was more mesmerized by her mouth or her eyes, wide silvery pools that reflected the same desire he felt. Then her long dark lashes swept closed, brushing the tops of her cheeks. Her high cheekbones and slim nose comprised a very patrician beauty. She could have been an empress in another time, yet he didn't even think she was aware of her power. She would have made slaves of men with her unaristocratic full-bodied laugh and incongruously pouty mouth.

Claiming that mouth with his own, he tasted her, nibbling slightly. He outlined her lips with the tip of his tongue, then withdrew before returning. They explored one another slowly. Not tentative in their actions, but patient, seeking, learning.

Her fingers threaded through his hair, a sensual massage against his scalp, and he cupped one hand behind the nape of her neck, drawing her closer. She opened her mouth beneath his, and their tongues met in a sweet friction that left him hard and aching. Using his weight, he guided her back to the wall behind them. Their kisses grew increasingly ravenous, only whetting his appetite for more instead of sating him.

Sharing his hunger, she moved restlessly, pushing her shoulders to the wall for leverage as she pressed against his erection. Need exploded inside him, and he dropped a hand to the outside of her thigh, squeezing through the denim and urging her to slide her leg upward. Her foot came to rest above his calf, and she lifted her hips to cradle him. The angle of their bodies was maddeningly intimate, but it wasn't enough.

He worked his fingers under her cropped sweater, across supple skin softer than the velvety knit covering it. Her body stilled for a moment, and Justin angled his head to deepen the kiss. He'd stop the instant she wanted him to, but until she decided that's what she wanted, he'd try his damnedest to convince her otherwise.

When Olivia wholeheartedly returned his kiss, he moved his hand farther up between their bodies. For days, he'd admired her lush womanly body, and now he wanted to claim each curve, show her how beautiful she was. He cupped her breast through the satiny fabric of her bra, almost groaning at the erotic feel of the hardened nipple beneath his hand.

Softly, barely grazing her, he brushed his thumb back and forth until she made a small sound in her throat and arched into his palm, seeking more. Her half moan, half whimper went straight through him, arrowing to his groin. How could this woman, who had his body on fire, have ever seemed aloof? No matter how cool her tone or demeanor, he'd never again be able to look at her without feeling this heat.

He broke off their kiss and bunched up the hem of her sweater. The chocolate-brown bra she wore was modest and ironically simple for someone who worked in the lingerie business, but Olivia hardly needed the artificial enhancement of push-up padding or frothy lace.

Pressing kisses in the smooth valley between her breasts, he hooked his thumb in her bra strap and tugged the material down enough to expose one pebbled coppery nipple. He ran his tongue over her, circling the sensitive tip before sucking gently. Olivia's grip on his arm tightened, and she rolled her shoulders back, curving upward to meet him. Overhead, a song he hadn't even consciously realized was playing ended, and her heart pounded in the momentary silence.

Bells literally rang in Justin's head as he turned to slide the other strap down her arm. It seemed that at one time, he'd been trying to make a point, but whatever it had been was far less important than the way Olivia had clung to him, returning his passion measure for measure.

Only she wasn't clinging anymore.

"J-Justin." She tapped his shoulder rather urgently. "Justin, wait!"

The bells sounded again, followed by a male voice from the intercom in the elevator panel. "This is Artie from maintenance, and we show your elevator's stopped operating. Everything okay in there? We tried the phone—"

Muttering a curse, Justin broke away from the swollen-lipped seductress in his arms and grabbed the red phone on the panel, assuring the man on the other end that they were fine.

"Got other people waiting for the elevators, you know," Artie chastised.

Behind Justin, Olivia muttered something, but it was hard to tell what over the blood still thundering in his ears.

"Sorry, we just stopped to, uh, get all our luggage loaded in," Justin improvised.

"Between floors?" Artie asked. "And are you finished with your *luggage?*"

He shot a glance at Olivia, who had pulled her bra up and her sweater down and was avoiding his eyes. Justin jabbed a button, and the elevator began moving again.

"We're finished."

But he feared his problems were only just beginning.

5

WHAT IN the *hell* had she just done?

Olivia squeezed her eyes shut as the elevator pitched into motion. Shame added warmth to her face, increasing her already feverish temperature. She'd heard of the Mile High Club—was there a club for people who'd almost done it between the twelfth and thirteenth floors?

It never would have gone that far. She wasn't that kind of person. Then again, how well did she really know herself? Because this morning she would have laughed at anyone who suggested she'd let Justin kiss her. If good old Artie hadn't called when he did, Justin would have had her shirt off in another two minutes—if she hadn't removed it herself to give him better access.

Feeling unpleasantly exposed, she started to fold her arms across her chest, but it was a little late for the extra barrier to do any good. Besides, her breasts were so sensitized she didn't want even the fabric of her bra brushing over them any more than necessary.

Aware Justin was looking in her direction, she cleared her throat and fought to regain her composure. "Well. That was about my worst nightmare ever." A searing loss of the self-discipline she'd fought so hard to build.

"Really?" He flashed a smile, making light of the situation. "Mine always involved being naked in front of a large group of people."

He was amused? Maybe this kind of thing happened to him all the time. Or maybe he just thought it was funny that it had happened to *her*, after her earlier—how had he put it?—self-righteousness.

"You don't seem like someone who would be embarrassed by public nudity," she said stiffly. Did elevators count as public? "You seem like a the-more-the-merrier kind of guy."

Speaking of elevators, why was this one still moving? They'd only had two floors left to go, one and a half if she wanted to get technical.

She might as well face disaster head-on, head off any gloating. "You obviously made your point. With gusto."

"What?" To his credit, there was nothing about his body language that said, "I told you so."

"I'm human, and I make mistakes." *And the understatement award goes to...* "Big mistakes."

"No, listen—"

"But I also learn from my mistakes, so this will not be happening again."

Olivia couldn't believe it had happened once! She'd been too curious and too aroused to deny herself this stolen chance to kiss him, but she was stunned at how quickly it—how quickly *she*—had spiraled out of control. Even though she enjoyed good sex, she rarely lost all sense of time, place and reason. Her first few experiences had not lived up to the lonely years of daydreaming that had preceded them, and though the encounters hadn't traumatized her, she was jaded enough now not to get swept away in mindless passion, either.

Mindless was a pretty accurate description for what had just taken place.

Finally, the elevator stopped. *Hallelujah.* Her entire body tensed in preparation for the moment those doors would slide open. She didn't care if she had to turn sideways and suck in her stomach to wiggle free, she was getting out of here.

As she stepped off, Justin reached out to stop her, and the simple contact of his fingers through her sleeve made her midsection clench. The throbbing need his kisses had stirred hadn't completely faded.

"Don't." She shrugged him away and kept moving forward.

"Olivia, I—"

A door to her left opened, and a female voice called out. "Justin, there you are!"

Wearing a tiny white robe and an expression of good-natured reprimand, Felicia emerged into the hallway. "I was thinking about going downstairs to look for you. Don't you know it's not nice to keep a girl waiting?"

Seeing Olivia, the model sighed. "But I guess you had work to do. Business before pleasure, right, Liv?"

Humiliation blazing through her, Olivia barely managed to nod. The whole time they were on the elevator, he'd had plans with the gorgeous model? Even though she knew she shouldn't look back, she glanced from the scantily clad woman back to Justin, who'd barely cleared the elevator doors.

He stood frozen in the hallway, his downward gaze

guilty. Olivia had thought she couldn't feel any worse about their moment of madness. She'd been wrong. The only saving grace was that Felicia didn't seem to notice anything amiss with Olivia's flushed and disheveled appearance.

Olivia resumed her escape, moving forward without really seeing where she was going. The door to her room almost came as a surprise. She fumbled with her key card, and, once inside, made a beeline for the bed.

No doubt Felicia and Justin were making a similar beeline, she thought as she sat at the end of the mattress. Despite her post-kiss bravado in stating that she didn't repeat mistakes, all evidence was pretty much to the contrary. First playboy Sean, now Justin.

Stormy, who had grown up on a farm, had once told Olivia that pigs were very smart. Given recent events, Olivia feared there might actually be *swine* out there grasping concepts faster than she was. Maybe it was odd to be thinking of pigs just now, but then again, after being manhandled by Justin Hawthorne, maybe not.

Liar. That had not been manhandling; that had been an unfinished seduction. And she'd been a willing participant. More fool, she.

Ticked off as she was at Justin, it wasn't as though an intelligent woman couldn't have guessed he had plans tonight. Olivia had spent the better part of the day watching him flirt with Felicia. With Stormy, too, for that matter. There was probably a kinky ménage à trois going on down the hall right now, but Olivia had ignored everything she'd seen with her own eyes in favor of playing tonsil hockey with the man.

Her face flamed, but the heat she felt wasn't just from anger, nor even completely from embarrassment. Much as she hated to admit it, she'd been more turned on than she'd ever been in her life. What would she have felt if they'd gone further, if he'd—

Learning curve, remember? If she was unwise enough to sit here and fantasize about the man, she might as well pad down the hall and see if they were interested in a foursome.

Exhaling a frustrated sigh, she forced herself to re-evaluate the situation logically. Justin wasn't down the hall having sex with anyone. At least, not yet. A man who kissed that thoroughly understood the benefits of exploration. And Felicia had mentioned going downstairs, so Olivia assumed she wore something underneath that robe. Justin couldn't be blamed for the model's state of dress, or relative lack thereof.

Also, it was highly unlikely that Stormy was with them. Even if Justin rotated the women in his bedroom the way conscientious drivers rotated tires, Olivia had a strong hunch that when he was with a woman, he focused solely and completely on her. As he had in the elevator. Heat spiraled back through her, and she had to remind herself calm logic was the order of the day.

The sad truth was, she'd waived her opportunity to do the sensible thing and stop him from kissing her. Stop him? She'd practically devoured him! So, despite the way she felt right now, an angry confrontation wouldn't be fair. It might also be a really bad idea, judging by the results of their *last* confrontation—results that still had her lips tingling.

His flirting with female colleagues aside, Justin was

great at his job. Olivia wanted to see Sweet Nothings grow, and losing him wouldn't help the company. Since neither of them was going anywhere, the best solution was to forget the kiss had ever happened.

Yeah.

She reached for the phone on the nightstand. If she didn't talk to someone soon, she might make another dumb-ass mistake tonight. Charge the entire contents of the minibar to her room, say.

Meg answered on the second ring. "'Lo?"

"Hey, Meggie. It's me." Olivia flopped back across the comforter. "This a bad time to talk?"

"Hell, no. You've saved me from cleaning my kitchen."

Olivia laughed. She knew from past experience that if her friend wanted to, she could repaint a room, do her taxes and speak into a cordless phone all at the same time.

"How'd it go on the beach?" Meg wanted to know.

"Better than it did in the elevator."

"You lost me."

Much as Olivia needed to vent, admitting what she'd done was tough. Best to work up to it. "Something happened the other night that I should mention...."

Olivia recounted seeing Justin with his sister, then today's events and the ensuing elevator confrontation.

"He kissed you?"

Holding the receiver away from her ear, Olivia blinked at her friend's volume. Obviously she'd shocked the unflappable Meg. "'Fraid so."

"You lucky devil!"

"*Lucky* isn't the word I'd use."

"Don't tell me a guy who looks like that is a lousy kisser. It would break my heart. Besides, you said someone from maintenance broke it up, so it doesn't sound like you were in any hurry to get away."

Olivia winced. "Sure, throw my own stupidity back at me."

"Are you kidding? This may be one of the better decisions you've made about men."

"Doubtful. I didn't get to the part where Felicia appeared in a robe and whisked him into her bedroom."

"Oh." Meg mulled over this new information. "So, you aren't having a beachfront fling with a hottie to exorcise Sean from your system and make a fresh start?"

"What? No! I told you, no men for me right now."

Silence. "Then why were you making out with Justin in an elevator?"

"Again I direct your attention to *stupidity*." Olivia barely refrained from thunking her forehead against the nightstand. "I have lousy taste in men."

"It's improving. Look, I've talked to Justin in the office. He may not be as much like Sean as you think."

"Right. Sean was covert about sleeping with other women."

"Do you really think he's sleeping with Felicia?" No need to specify that she meant Justin and not Sean.

Oddly, Olivia thought she'd be bothered less by her ex-boyfriend with the model than the man she'd only known a few days. How bizarre was that?

"I don't know, Meg." When she contemplated what might be going on several rooms away, a pain stabbed behind her right eye. "He confuses the hell out of me.

The day I met him, I jumped to the conclusion he was as bad as the rest of them, but later decided I'd misjudged him. But when I saw him having dinner with that gorgeous blonde—"

"His sister? Genetics must've been kind to that family."

No question, the man wore his genes well. "Then there was that fight this evening—"

"And the kiss," Meg added, sounding breathless on her friend's behalf.

"Uh, yeah. And now—"

"Felicia."

"In a nutshell. It really shouldn't matter what he's doing, though." Or who. "He's wrong for me for about a dozen reasons. But even if he were miraculously right, I'm not getting involved with a co-worker during a promotion evaluation period." Not that Sweet Nothings didn't have its share of juicy relationship drama— half the people around her acted as if they were starring in their own Aaron Spelling show—but Olivia was trying to prove herself.

"Guess I can't argue with you," Meg said, sounding as though she'd very much like to try. "So the plan is what, exactly?"

"Get a ride back with Rick tomorrow and never mention that kiss again."

A much better plan than her earlier minibar thought—longer-lasting, hangover free and easy to execute. She guessed that Justin was no more anxious to discuss tonight's gaffe than she was. Men were *never* the ones who wanted to talk.

JUSTIN STEPPED out of the line at the hotel's registration desk, purposefully inserting himself in Olivia's path. "We need to talk."

Smooth, man. What happened to the diplomatic approach you had all planned out?

He'd had plenty of time to plan after he'd exchanged hot-tubbing with Felicia for a solo cold shower. She'd shrugged off his rejection with a bewildered your-loss attitude, then gone downstairs alone, though he doubted she'd lacked company for long. *He* should have been that company, but haunted by the stricken look of self-disgust on Olivia's face, he'd paced his room, deliberating what to say the next time he saw her.

The "next time" had been this morning's pool shoot, hardly the place for a chat. Unlike yesterday on the beach, when Olivia had been remote, today she'd praised his work and taken pains—literally, he was sure—to smile at him. But she'd been nervous, which was made apparent by the manic dipping of her tea bag in the ceramic hotel mug whenever she forced herself to talk to him. Judging by the way she'd furtively ducked into the bustling lobby seconds ago from a side stairwell, she was still nervous.

If she wanted to go unnoticed, she should've worn something other than the mint-green knit dress and little matching shirt jacket. On someone else, the ankle-length sheath might have been shapeless, but on Olivia's body, it was a gently clinging cotton ode to her generous breasts and hips. As soon as she'd sensed Justin's gaze on her, she'd bolted with the speed and grace of a nervous doe toward Rick, who was several people ahead of Justin in the checkout line.

And that was when Justin inserted himself in Olivia's path and rashly announced they needed to talk.

"About that kiss," he added, silently daring her to try to forget. She could call it a mistake, but she couldn't will it out of existence.

"Here?" The impassioned spark in her eyes, even if it stemmed from anger, made him want to kiss her again.

Who was he kidding? Her breathing made him want to kiss her again.

"You want to talk about it *here?*" She waved her hand in an annoyed gesture that indicated the half-dozen people in the lobby who were affiliated with Sweet Nothings. "Sure you don't want to wait for a more appropriate time and location? A staff meeting, maybe?"

"Well, we could discuss it in the privacy of the car," he offered, "but somehow I got the impression you were planning to ask someone else for a ride back." Someone like Rick.

She nibbled on her lower lip. "I'm not sure why we should discuss it at all."

Her words confirmed what he'd already guessed. She wanted to disregard what had happened. The thought bothered him more than he liked, but he told himself it was because pretending it had never happened would only lead to avoidance and awkwardness. This morning had already proven that, and he wanted to get past this so he could fully enjoy his new job. They needed to clear the air.

Keeping her away from Rick and his unnaturally blinding grins was just a bonus.

"Ride with me," he told her. "Give me an opportunity to apologize." *Opportunity* being the keyword. He wasn't sure he could bring himself to say he was sorry for what they'd shared.

"How 'bout I just accept your apology now and see you back at the office?" She glanced anxiously over his shoulder to where Rick chatted with one of the stylists.

Rick draped his arm around the woman he was talking to, and Justin mentally rolled his eyes. All morning the makeup artist had flirted poolside with Felicia, and while Justin had been relieved the model had a new admirer, why wasn't Olivia chastising *Rick* for his hound-dog ways?

Not that I'm jealous. "I need to know that we can work together with this truly behind us," he said.

"We can."

"The drive to Atlanta will prove that."

Her eyebrows shot up, her apprehensive expression replaced by an almost endearing scowl. "I don't have to prove anything to you."

"Of course not," he agreed quickly. Life with sisters had taught him when to sound conciliatory. "I wasn't challenging you. I was trying to help. You know, the get-back-up-on-the-horse philosophy."

"And you're the horse?" Pink stained her cheeks, but she lifted her chin and defiantly plowed on with the unfortunate analogy. "Trust me, getting on you is not the answer."

The brief yet powerful image of Olivia astride him left him temporarily unable to form words. Even more arousing was the certainty that she'd had a similar mental picture. Her eyes widened, and her lips parted. The memory of last night's encounter roared to life between them, blazing with sensual promise.

For a moment, Justin almost said to hell with his job and pulled her against him here and now.

He cleared his throat. "I, uh...I just thought that dealing with me now would be more comfortable for you in the long run than postponing—"

"You're worried that *I'll* be too uncomfortable?"

This was where he should be saying yes, but something in her eyes made him hesitate.

"What about you, Justin? No chance of discomfort on your part?" She took a predatory step closer, her expression provocative. Apparently, she'd decided not to care about the co-workers scattered among brass luggage carts and upholstered benches. "I'd hate to think I didn't make an impression."

She wasn't touching him, but she lowered her gaze and took a leisurely visual tour that caused him to stiffen.

He kept his voice low. "If you'd like, I could show you how much of an impression you made...are making now."

Blinking with the same sort of bemused surprise a person feels upon waking and discovering it was only a dream, she leaned back, inserting distance between them without moving her feet. "I'm sorry. That was—"

Sexy as hell.

"—inappropriate. I don't know why I behaved that way."

He did. He'd felt some of it himself when she'd headed in Rick's direction. The need to remind her of what had passed between them, the need to assert his claim on her.

Maybe she was right. Sharing a vehicle for the next few hours might not be such a good idea.

She sighed. "Okay, I'm in. We should ride back together."

"What?" There was no winning with this woman.

"I think being in your company will be a good reminder."

Of what, exactly? That the chemistry they shared hovered between the explosive and the sublime? Somehow, he doubted that was what she'd meant.

Moving toward the counter, she shook her head. "Looks like we're doing things your way."

Hardly. He watched her from behind, appreciating the subtle cling of the fabric as it fell from the line of her back across the curve of her butt. *His* way wouldn't involve checking out or driving back to Atlanta at all. His way would be to take Olivia upstairs to one of the hotel's king-size beds and keep her there until both of them were so limp with satisfaction that it would be all they could do to dial up room service.

Damn shame they weren't doing things his way.

6

OLIVIA SQUIRMED in the passenger seat, hoping Justin hadn't noticed how fidgety she was. She couldn't decide if her jumpiness was nerves or sexual tension. Worse, she couldn't even tell if it was Justin who made her nervous or her own unpredictable behavior—such as hitting on him back in the hotel lobby.

Although, maybe it had been more sexually baiting, behavior of which she was not proud. The possibility that he'd been unaffected by their kiss had provoked her in a manner that was completely un-Olivia.

The good news was, he hadn't slept with Felicia. The model had paid him almost zero notice this morning, and Olivia knew intuitively that no woman would simply be able to dismiss Justin after a night of passion. A smart woman probably wouldn't even let him out of bed. Felicia had barely spared him a sulky glance before returning to her usual gregarious self and laughing with Rick, who'd offered to give her a lift to the city once Olivia had changed her plans.

She and Justin passed a series of blue Exit signs that listed lodgings and restaurants, and he angled his chin at the familiar logo of a world-famous fast-food chain. "Any chance you want a milk shake?"

"A milk shake?" She couldn't help laughing at the

spontaneous offer. "And here I thought *coffee* was the adult drink of choice for everyone but me."

"Guess I developed a milk shake addiction after using them to smooth over any rough times with my sisters. Plus, I want something cold."

"In early March?" The predicted cold front had indeed moved in. Outside her window, wind whipped the limbs of dogwood trees, and the sky was a sunless stale gray.

He took his eyes off the road just long enough to glance pointedly in her direction, not bothering to mask the barely banked desire in his expression. "I could use some cooling off, yeah."

Gulp. "I'll take a diet soda."

A few minutes later, Justin handed Olivia her soft drink. Their fingers brushed, and the fleeting contact was enough to make her suck in her breath. She'd lain awake most of the night, reliving the feel of those capable fingers on her.

He sipped his large strawberry shake, then made a sound of low appreciation that caused her skin to tingle. "Not bad."

If he derived that much pleasure from something "not bad," she didn't think she could endure his enjoyment of anything that actually ranked good or higher.

"You sure you don't want some?" he offered.

Oh, she wanted some all right. "I don't eat ice cream."

"Ever?" He sounded appalled. "Is it a lactose thing?"

It was an ex-fat-girl thing. "No, just me watching my

figure." She said it rebelliously, still annoyed by his accusation that she had "hang-ups."

Wanting to be able to zip her jeans was *not* a neurosis, and she was proud of the willpower she'd cultivated. Even if said willpower had been noticeably absent yesterday evening.

"I'll make you a deal," Justin said. "You have the ice cream, and *I'll* watch your figure."

"You just watch the road."

"Okay." He lifted the milk shake once again, and his cheeks hollowed as he sucked on the straw. Her body burned with the memory of those lips on her breast, drawing her nipple into the satiny warmth of his mouth.

A few minutes later, he added, "You don't know what you're missing."

Frustration that had nothing to do with dairy desserts raked through her. "Why are you trying to sabotage my self-discipline?"

"You mean self-denial? Letting go occasionally can be healthy, too. Would one sip really hurt anything?"

No. In fact, some dieticians said that "controlled cheating" was a good thing because a person who felt they'd been deprived too long was more prone to bingeing.

"If I take a sip, will you leave me alone?"

He flashed her a wicked grin. "I make no promises."

Somehow she was unsurprised. "Just give me the damn shake."

The sweetness of strawberries melted on her tongue like summer-flavored snowflakes, and Olivia shivered at the unexpected indulgence. When was the last time she'd allowed any form of ice cream to pass her lips? Then again, her lips seemed to have lost all restraint these days.

"Good, isn't it?" he asked.

"Mmm. I haven't had one in years."

"So you weren't kidding about it not being a grown-up drink."

"It's just that..." She did not want to discuss how overweight she'd once been, how her mom had expressed love through baking and how potato chips had eased the sting of not going to school dances. "Earlier you said sisters, plural. How many do you have? I'm an only child myself."

His sidelong glance was assessing, but he went along with the redirection. "Two. Lisa, who's at Auburn, and Andrea, whom you saw the other night. Apparently."

Traces of mortification lingered as she recalled how she'd wrongly confronted him. "About that...I apologize, again, for jumping to conclusions."

"Don't worry." Mischief laced his tone. "I stopped being angry about that pretty fast. It's hard to stay mad when—"

"It's just that I'm coming off a bad breakup," she blurted, desperately wanting to cut off whatever he'd been about to say. Her loss of control was embarrassing enough without the reminders. "So I've been a little cynical lately, but I shouldn't have taken it out on you."

He was quiet for a moment. "You know what I hear is helpful? A transitional guy, someone you can use briefly to get over your heartache. If you're looking for someone you can exploit sexually..."

"I'm not." But it was hard to keep from laughing. Justin was exactly the kind of sexy charmer she should stay away from, but it was difficult not to enjoy his company. "You aren't going to keep doing this, are you?"

"Doing what, offering useful suggestions?"

She sent a halfhearted glare his way, then drank more of the strawberry milk shake.

"Am I getting that back?"

"Depends on how much you irritate me."

He chuckled, but then his tone turned unexpectedly serious. "I am sorry to hear about the rough breakup. If you want to talk, we've got plenty of time in the car and, trust me, I've got practice listening."

She almost dismissed the offer out of hand, but his offer of a friendly ear sounded genuine. During his short time at Sweet Nothings, she'd been aloof more often than not, and maybe she owed him a brief explanation.

"I dated a guy for a few months," she said, "thought we were getting fairly serious until I came home from a cancelled meeting and found him doing the mattress mambo with my roommate."

"You're joking." His tone was one of outraged bewilderment, which Olivia found amusing in a sad kind of way. She didn't think infidelity was so rare as to be puzzling.

"If I was joking, I would have started off 'A politician walks into a bar...'"

Her attempt to laugh away the subject didn't alter

Justin's scowl. "I can't understand the guy's problem. The obvious fact that he's an ass aside, you'd more than keep a man happy in bed."

Liquid heat suffused her body, starting in her chest, near her heart, and spreading through her veins. "You don't know that. Maybe I'm awful."

What is wrong with me? Why hadn't she just mumbled "thanks" or, better yet, ignored the comment?

He snorted. "Awful, with your passion? Not a chance. You can try to hide it behind clothes that cover you from neck to ankle and a refusal to taste anything even halfway decadent, but I know—"

"No, you don't." So much for the warm fuzzies. His presumptuousness set her teeth on edge. "It was just a kiss, that doesn't imbue you with magical insight."

"It wasn't 'just' anything, sweetheart." He turned his head toward her, his eyes erotically intense. "And try looking at it from the other side, if you don't believe me. Are you honestly saying you couldn't make a few educated guesses about my performance now?"

Flames licked through her blood. On the job, her vibrant visualization skills served her well, but all they were helping with now was raising the temperature inside the car.

Justin sliding the straps of her bra down her shoulders, kissing her exposed skin...lowering her to a mattress, covering her body with his weight...kissing her as she straddled him, their tongues tangled in wanton exploration.

She wanted to tell him that his *performance* was none of her concern, but if she opened her mouth to speak, the words *take me* would spill out of their own volition.

At least she knew he wasn't unaffected, either. His hands were clenched on the steering wheel in a death grip, and his gaze was so fixed on the road that she expected to see tiny holes appear in the windshield.

Even though she'd recounted what had happened between her and Sean, she felt none of the previous incensed bitterness that mentioning her ex had conjured in the past. In fact, she could barely recall his face right now.

She swallowed, wanting to get the conversation on a less volatile topic. "I appreciate your, ah, vote of confidence, but it's okay, really. I don't even miss him that much."

After a brief silence, Justin said, "I know it sounds like a cliché, but he didn't deserve you."

The sincerity in his voice had a bittersweet effect. She didn't need any more reasons to like Justin. What she needed was an ejection button and cab fare to Atlanta.

Smiling to show she was only kidding, she said, "You're right. That is a cliché."

"But they become clichés because they're true. There's someone better out there, probably looking for you."

Out there, he'd been careful to specify, as in definitely not in this car.

"Well, he'll have to wait until after I get this promotion," she said, shooting for a breezy tone. "*If* I get this promotion, but then...I'm going to be more careful next time. Find myself a nice solid settling-down kind of guy."

"Sounds good. I mean, if you're into relationships."

"I gather from your barely repressed shudder that you aren't?" she asked dryly.

He grimaced. "I'm more interested in having a good time than seeing someone I have to call if I'm gonna be late. Guess I'm one of those guys who's still trying to work out all that selfish me-time."

Since he wasn't telling her anything she hadn't already deduced, she didn't know why she felt such a stab of disappointment. She knew what she needed— Mr. Reliable. Not someone who unexpectedly stopped elevators and had her clothes askew moments later, someone who winked at models and sixty-year-olds alike and would leave her once again questioning if any of that flirtation translated to cheating, someone who had her eating ice cream, for crying out loud!

Nope, she didn't want someone like that at all.

"So?" Meg demanded on the other end of the phone.

Olivia curled and uncurled the spiral cord around her hand as she stood at the navy-blue kitchen counter and waited for the microwave to beep. "So...what?"

"Nice try. Last night, you call all hot and bothered over this guy, then today you spend hours alone with him in the car and pretend to have *nothing* to report? Don't make me come over there and kick your skinny butt."

"Getting less skinny every second. You'll be happy to know I had a milk shake earlier, or at least part of one. And frankly..." She wrinkled her nose at the unappealing low-cal meal she'd dutifully heated. There had to be more to life than choosing your food based on caloric value. "I'm considering ordering a pizza."

A small shriek came over the line. Either Meg's astonishment defied articulation, or there was a parakeet in distress. "First ice cream and now pizza? Are you serious?"

"I think so." Olivia was suddenly too aware of the lack of sensory pleasure she let herself experience. "You have dinner plans already? I'll feel less guilty if I don't eat alone." Not to mention she would have a distraction from dwelling on Justin Hawthorne all night.

In theory.

An hour later, Meg was seated in one of the padded bamboo chairs at the kitchen table, using a napkin to clean her fingers. Olivia sat perched atop the kitchen counter, swinging her legs back and forth pendulum-style and battling pizza buyer's remorse. Justin had been the featured topic of conversation, even after Olivia's refusal to share any more details of what had transpired on the elevator.

"He has you necking while on a professional shoot *and* polishing off four pieces of pizza?" Meg marveled. "He's clearly not human."

Olivia chuckled dryly. "So what's your theory exactly? Evil, here from another dimension to tempt us?"

"Nah." Meg waggled her eyebrows. "I was thinking sex god."

That actually didn't seem far-fetched. "So I had a little pizza for once. I just felt like it, it has nothing to do with Justin."

"Uh-huh."

"You're my best friend. Couldn't you at least *pretend* to believe me? I need my dignity, Meg."

Standing, Meg pitched her empty paper plate atop

Olivia's in the likewise empty pizza box. "Dignity isn't going to keep you warm on long winter nights."

"Then it's a good thing we're coming into spring, because I'm gonna concentrate on work for now. Get that promotion, and buy a sofa for the gaping empty hole in my living room."

She had to admit, though, that ever since driving home after Justin dropped her off at the office, she hadn't been able to shake the feeling that there was a gaping empty hole in her *life*. Perhaps that was normal after a breakup, but she had trouble believing the emptiness had been left by Sean. She saw her parents almost once a month, but had never introduced Sean to them. Wouldn't she have, if she'd ever really believed she might love him? Truth be told, in her reflective moments, she missed the ex-roommate more than the ex-boyfriend.

"Meg, can I ask you something?"

Refilling her drink in front of the open refrigerator, Meg nodded. "Fire away."

"What did I see in Sean? I mean, sure we hit it off okay one night at a party, and he had his moments. But enough to justify six months of my life?"

Meg looked down, obviously taking a moment to arrange her thoughts. Since her friend was generally quick with an opinion, the hesitation made Olivia uneasy—as though she'd asked something she didn't really want answered.

"I assume you mean beyond his hotness? Because that would be the easy response."

Sean had been inarguably gorgeous, but Olivia couldn't remember a time when his appearance had caused the internal tremor that seeing Justin did. "Yeah, beyond that."

"Well...safety, I guess."

"What?" Olivia lost track of the unconscious rhythm of her swinging legs and winced when she banged her left calf against the cabinet handle below her.

"From what you've said and what you haven't, I gather high school and college were not easy times for you."

"They're probably not easy for anyone," Olivia hedged.

High school had been a dateless existence. Her last two years of college had provided both dates and disillusionment. Carelessly eager to share her heart with someone, she'd made some bad choices.

Meg shook her head, not fooled by Olivia's attempt to sound dismissive. "I think you gravitate toward guys like Sean because—"

"I'm still trying to prove I'm not that fat unattractive girl anymore?" She slid down off the counter, depressed with her character.

"No. You aren't that shallow. Or that needy. I was going to say you pick casual heartbreakers because they're easier on you in the long run. Nine times out of ten, things don't work out, but it's not like you really get hurt."

"You don't think it upset me to find him in bed with another woman?"

"Upset, sure. Ticked off, even. And majorly inconvenienced when you ended up without someone to split the rent. But I don't think you're all that stricken to see him go."

Catching her bottom lip between her teeth, Olivia realized she'd probably chewed off all her lipstick hours ago. Bad habit, but better than nervous cookie consumption. "You know what? I was just thinking that I miss Candace more than I do Sean. You're wise beyond your years."

"Well, it is easier to be wise about someone *else's* life."

The kitchen and living room were really one large rectangle, divided into two squares where the cream carpet met gold-flecked linoleum. Meg walked into the next "room," glancing nostalgically at the area where, on previous visits, she'd made herself comfy on the couch.

"You can take the armchair," Olivia offered.

"What about you?"

"I thought I'd pace in useless sexual frustration."

Meg laughed, but her expression turned sagelike again as she warmed to her role as Imparter of Wisdom. "After guys like Sean, it's easy to understand why Justin has you in emotional uproar."

"It's not my emotions that are roaring. It's my hormones."

"You don't fool me. This is a man who's not just sexy, but funny and caring. You could actually lose your heart to him."

Oh, no. Olivia had learned that lesson. Learned it, majored in it, graduated magna cum laude. "Caring? You've known the guy a week, Meg."

"Hey, you deal with the layout end of the catalog, I deal with people. I know what I'm talking about. Have you ever seen how nice he is to Ms. Phipps? And Judy in accounting had her little girl in the office Wednesday, and you should have seen him with her. He was a natural."

"Well, he did grow up with sisters," Olivia muttered, trying not to remember the way he'd sincerely asked about her breakup and offered to listen. He'd teased and flirted with her throughout their ride to Atlanta, but he hadn't done anything inappropriate when he'd said goodbye to her in the deserted parking garage. He'd merely opened her door for her and then waited until she had the car running to follow her back onto the main street.

But he didn't strike her as someone looking to settle into the sensible committed relationship she'd promised herself. He'd made plans with Felicia and was having dinner with Kate, and those were only the dates Olivia *knew* about.

"Sorry, Meg, but in this case your wisdom's a little off the mark. There's nothing between me and Justin."

Her friend opened her mouth, probably to bring up that elevator kiss, so Olivia hastily amended, "Okay, from here on out, there's nothing between me and Justin."

Meg pursed her lips. "We'll see."

7

Justin was passing through the executive reception area on Monday morning when Diane's voice stopped him.

"What's your hurry?" The sultry redhead practically purred the question.

His hurry was a new boss to impress and an appointment with Steve to go over a CD of digital pictures from the beach shoot. But Justin paused for a moment anyway, determined to regain his focus on a new life—the kind of life that centered around his enjoying himself, not turning away gorgeous women because he was preoccupied with someone else. The kind of life he'd earned.

Over the weekend, he'd gone out with some buddies from Hilliard, but, while it had been nice to come home at whatever hour he felt like, his social life still needed a woman's touch. Unfortunately, he'd spent too many hours thinking about touching Olivia Lockhart. In a perfect world, they could have a scorching affair that would cure his lust for her, then part amicably. But she'd said flat-out that she was looking for stability, and he'd had a bellyful of that these last few years. Time to shake things up a little, be more like Bryan.

He glanced over his shoulder to smile at Diane, who was en route back to her desk, several manila folders in her extravagantly manicured hand. How did she type with nails that long? "'Morning. Hope you had a good weekend."

"It was okay." Her azure eyes raked over his body with unconcealed appreciation. "Definitely could have been better, with the right company."

She took a step forward, murmuring a soft "excuse me" as she brushed her body against his to get to the desk on the other side of him. Beyond the desk, Steve's door was shut.

"He's in a meeting." Diane settled into her rolling office chair. "But he shouldn't be long. You can keep me company."

He sat on the black leather love seat opposite her desk, sparing a cursory glance at the trendily shaped trapezoid table and its array of fashion magazines and catalog back issues. "How long have you worked for Sweet Nothings?"

"Long enough to get all my lingerie at a great employee discount. I have quite the collection." Her smile was so brazen, he wouldn't have been surprised if she rolled up the hem of her gauzy black skirt to show off garter-clipped stockings.

He'd always applauded women who made the first move, and Diane was undeniably striking. Yet he felt the same way now as he had about a month ago, when he'd gone to a traveling photography display at the High Museum. He'd been able to appreciate the aesthetic value of the exhibits even as he knew they weren't really to his taste.

"Of course, sometimes," Diane confided, a wicked

note in her voice, "I find underwear to be superfluous, don't you?"

"*Ahem.*"

Justin lifted his gaze to the now-open door behind Diane's desk. Steve was in the background, speaking into his phone, but Olivia stood scowling in the doorway. Who would have guessed he could be so attracted to a woman wearing a disgruntled expression and a baggy muted violet sweater with darker slacks? The color was flattering to her black hair and lighter eyes, but did she really have to be covered up from the tips of her boot-style shoes to the cowl neck of her top?

He couldn't shake the impression that she was trying to hide herself, but maybe he was reading too much into a random clothing choice. Wearing a sweater in March wasn't exactly out of the ordinary, and Olivia wasn't a timid woman. Witness the times she'd given him a piece of her mind.

She looked ready to do so now.

He grinned unrepentantly at her. He hadn't asked for Diane's panty past. Besides, sometimes underwear *was* superfluous.

"'Morning, Olivia."

"'Morning." Her smoky gaze met his, but she looked away almost immediately.

"Liv, wait!" Behind her, Steve hung up the phone and crossed his office. "I know you need to talk to Meg to confirm B and B models, but why don't you stay a few more minutes and look at Justin's prelim shots with us? It'll save you and me another meeting later."

Justin couldn't help catching her eye—they both knew how she felt about meetings with Steve. Her lips twitched in an answering smile, and the gratified rush it gave him was heady. A man could get addicted to wanting to see her happy.

Steve stepped to the side, ushering both of them in before calling to his receptionist, "Diane, how about rustling us up a pitcher of coffee and three mugs?"

The receptionist stood. "Sure."

"Olivia doesn't drink coffee."

Three heads turned in Justin's direction, three faces wearing matching surprised expressions. Then Olivia's grin brightened. Did she have any idea how beautiful smiling like that made her, any idea that she could scatter his thoughts with a simple movement of her mouth?

He nearly groaned. He'd never get through this informal presentation if he was thinking about her mouth.

Steve glanced at Olivia, eyebrows raised. "No coffee?"

She shook her head. "No, thank you."

"Is there something else you'd like?" Steve asked.

Tea. Justin almost smiled, recalling how she'd sip the warm beverage when she was stalling before answering a question and the way she fidgeted with the tea bag when she was nervous.

Olivia shook her head a second time. "I'm good."

Good was an understatement, Justin thought as he followed them into Steve's darkly paneled office. The heavy mahogany furniture, leather armchairs and stereotypically macho color scheme suggested that there should be aged Scotch at a side bar and hunting trophies mounted on the walls. Instead, framed Sweet

Nothings covers hung on the wood paneling, and, from every side of the room, lingerie-clad models beckoned with seductive smiles. The overall decorating effect was Hemingway meets Hefner.

Steve sat behind his desk, and Justin and Olivia took the two chairs opposite him. "So, Liv, your first time being in charge of a shoot, and your first job for us, Justin. How did it go? Smoothly?"

Smooth as a baby porcupine's bottom.

"I'll let the pictures answer for themselves," Justin evaded.

"Spoken like a true photographer. Liv, anything you want to add?"

She glanced at Justin, and for a moment he thought she'd look away nervously, as she'd done when she'd first seen him in the outer office.

He grinned in challenge.

Her eyes narrowed, and she kept her gaze locked with his, rising to the unspoken dare. "Justin was, um, surprising, at times, but it's obvious he has quite a bit of experience. And even though we have to factor in budget and outdoor conditions, I'm happy to say he doesn't rush or do things halfheartedly."

Good for her, he thought laughingly. "I do like to do a thorough job. And I'm willing to take direction. If I left you unsatisfied in any way, you should come down to the studio and we can explore some different approaches. I'm just an elevator ride away."

Color bloomed in her cheeks. "I'm sure that won't be necessary."

"Sounds promising," Steve said, inserting the CD in the computer.

A knock sounded at the door, and Diane brought in a carafe of coffee on a small tray with two mugs, sugar and creamer. Justin poured his black, and waited as Steve prepared his. With that accomplished, Steve swiveled his computer monitor so they could all get a better look.

"Obviously, the ones we think we'll be using will be presented at the design meeting later," their supervisor said. "Along with the film photographs. But I wanted to take a peek at these shots with you two to get a feel for how things are going."

They went through several pictures, some of which Justin felt could have been better, but no one seemed unhappy with his work. Steve clicked the mouse, enlarging a thumbnail of Stormy in an ice-blue bikini. She was walking on the beach, her body angled toward the water.

Justin was proud of this one, of the sense of motion and the expression he'd captured. She wasn't smiling, which sometimes appeared posed even when it was natural, but nor was she projecting that ultraserious supposedly seductive look models were taught. Instead, her eyes twinkled with playfulness. Sexy enough to make any man look twice, but approachable enough that women would relate, see Stormy as the slightly wicked friend they secretly wanted to be more like. It was a good picture with real commercial value.

His gaze shifted slightly to Olivia, who was studying the digital image. Not for the first time, he thought how much he'd like to photograph her. Could he capture on film what he saw in her, despite the conservative clothes and occasional prickly moments?

Learning about her unfaithful ex-boyfriend this weekend had certainly explained some of that prickliness. He recalled her flippant comment about sex in the car. *Maybe I'm awful.* Although she hadn't meant it literally, Justin imagined being cheated on wasn't beneficial to anyone's self-esteem. He couldn't help feeling she sometimes underestimated herself.

She looked up, seeming startled to find him watching her. "This picture especially works. The models, um, really responded to you."

"Thanks." He'd had fun, too. What man wouldn't want to spend an afternoon filming gorgeous women playing up to him? But it hadn't felt as good as Olivia against him as he kissed her breathless.

"I'm pleased to hear about the model-photographer chemistry," Steve interjected. "It looks like Fred might not be back in time for the B and B shoot next Tuesday."

Compassion etched little worry lines around Olivia's silvery eyes. "Is his sister doing all right?"

"Yes, according to his e-mail. She just underestimated how long it would take to get back to full strength." Steve made a dismissive gesture with one hand, moving the mouse with his other. "Justin, I'd like you to do the shoot—it's an important one, here at a bed-and-breakfast in Atlanta. Olivia's familiar with the space and has already been storyboarding layout ideas, so the two of you will be doing this together."

Olivia blinked, then smiled, her expression the kind that looked stilted and artificial in pictures. "Great. We'll discuss specifics later this week, but now I really should get together with Meg and confirm the models.

We've booked Veronica for the June catalog, but there was some worry about a conflict in Stormy's schedule. I want to make sure we've got Tony, too."

Standing, she glanced awkwardly in Justin's direction. "I guess I'll be seeing you next Tuesday. I mean, sooner than that of course, I just...our second shoot, and all..."

"I got it." Justin grinned. The woman was cute when she was flustered. Very kissable.

If it were up to him, they'd be kissing again soon. But could he get what he thought they both wanted without giving up the new found freedom he needed?

OLIVIA PAUSED outside the ground-level studio, taking a deep breath and holding the sketches to the front of her body like a shield—a really useless paper shield with rough drawings of faceless people in their underwear. By four-thirty, many employees had already ducked out to try to beat evening traffic, but there was still a chance someone would see her here, looking like an idiot. Not to mention feeling like one. It wasn't as if she hadn't seen Justin every day this week already... although she had managed to avoid being alone with him until now.

This was asinine. It was already Wednesday, and they needed to talk about the layout of the bed-and-breakfast and the pictures for the Father's Day catalog, which would feature more than the usual posed women modeling the products. There would be sexy scenes of couples that showed off his-and-her robes and men's silk boxer shorts, gift ideas and romantic tableaus that encouraged women to surprise their husbands by wearing seductive lingerie.

Which meant Olivia would be spending most of next Tuesday cooped up in a bedroom with Justin. No big deal. She was a professional.

A fact that would be easier to prove when she stopped hovering in the hallway.

Chin raised, she marched into the studio. "Hello?"

The click of a shutter answered before he did. "Give me just a sec. I'm almost finished here."

The downstairs space was a wide room split into different areas of use. First was the small officelike section Fred used when he was here. It included a rather beat-up desk with its computer and phone system and a single chair. Then came the "tabletop studio" where Justin stood now. Beyond that, the larger area used for Web site shots, "export" ads for billboards and magazine placement, and the smaller stock photos in the catalog, such as images accompanying a bra layout that showed the different ways the straps could be worn.

The table housed all kinds of complicated electronic equipment, and Justin had set up an area to photograph a colorful array of lace against a soft gray background that would show up white in the picture. When she got closer, she realized the frothy pile of material on the table was panty samples from the Unlimited Curves line. A piece of the lingerie was always featured on a model, but there would also be a photo insert showing different color choices.

She paused by Fred's desk, a safe distance away. "I could come back another time if you're busy."

Justin flashed a knowing grin over his shoulder. "Running off so soon?"

"No, being respectful of your schedule."

"Like I said, almost finished. Besides, I'm just running a test sheet to check the filters, make sure the colors are coming through right." He switched off the lamp standing near the table and walked toward her.

"You can take the seat," he offered.

There was only one real office chair. Against the backdrop on the other side of the room, there was a chaise lounge that had been used for an ad, and wouldn't that just be a cozy place for the two of them to sit and look at the drawings?

"I'll stand."

"Sorry about the limited options. They're supposed to be moving some more furniture down here." He slid a portfolio of sample fashion-show shots aside and leaned casually on the edge of Fred's desk.

She and Justin had passed each other in the halls this week and even sat across from one another at meetings, but this was the first time he'd been so close. She wanted to move away, but he'd notice. Being him, he'd probably even comment.

It was the end of the day, and he'd been working with the studio lights. Instead of the scent of store-bought cologne, there was only earthy, rugged male— far more tantalizing than a bottled fragrance mixed in some lab. The man was a feast for the five senses. The sight of him, the way he smelled, the timbre of his bedroom voice...she couldn't help but imagine touching him. Tasting him.

"I understand all about limited seating," she babbled, needing something safe to focus on. "I don't have a couch. I mean, not in my office—well, of course not in my office, why would I need a couch in my tiny office—but I don't actually have one in my apartment, either. I did, or my roommate did, but..." She put the brakes on her runaway thoughts, but not in time to stem the embarrassing display of mangled oratory.

She dropped her sketches on the desk, resisting the urge to hide behind her hands. "You should've just stopped me."

His smile was wicked. "Any particular preference on how?"

No way she was answering that. "I swear you're the only person who makes me ramble like an idiot."

"That's flattering."

"It's annoying as all hell."

"Would it help if I said I don't think you're an idiot?"

That made one of them.

Though Justin looked amused, at least he didn't come off as laughing at her, which she appreciated. His demeanor seemed more affectionate than condescending, and she felt the same warmth toward him she'd felt when he'd remembered her preference for tea. A tiny thing, sure, but in the months she'd been with Sean, the confirmed caffeine dependent, he'd always turned to her expectantly at the end of the meal when a waiter asked if they wanted coffee.

That had been the problem with her ex-boyfriend, not just the way he'd looked at other women, but the way he'd managed not to see her. Justin not only focused on her, he often made her feel as if no one else existed but the two of them. Too bad he had no interest in a relationship—he'd probably be better at it than her last boyfriend.

Olivia had been silent for a long moment, and Justin wondered what she was thinking. He knew what *he'd* been thinking about all day—her.

He'd seen her when he headed for a meeting earlier, and she'd stayed on his mind throughout the discussion of the upcoming Sweet Nothings fashion show. He was pretty sure he'd been assigned some runway pictures, but they could have asked him to take pictures of a driveway and he wouldn't have noticed. When he'd arranged lingerie for test shots this afternoon, he couldn't help but imagine Olivia in the slinky delicate garments—better yet, out of them.

She probably wasn't here now because of similar fantasies.

"What can I do for you, Liv?" *Or to you?*

She made a face as if someone had tried to get her to eat brussel sprouts. "Don't call me that, for starters."

"Oh. Sure." He felt strangely wounded, and he didn't even *like* the abbreviated version of her name. "We're not really close enough for nicknames, are we?" Ironic, since they'd been about as close as two fully clothed people could get.

Her chuckle surprised him. "It isn't that. To tell you the truth, I hate 'Liv.' I just got tired of reminding Steve, and the name caught on."

The explanation, and her accompanying smile, immediately melted away the hollow coldness of rejection. "Duly noted. For what it's worth, 'Liv' doesn't suit you, anyway."

"No?" She looked inordinately cheered by this. She must really hate the nickname.

"Olivia's better...has a rhythm."

"Rhythm?"

Did she even realize she'd leaned slightly closer? He was aware of every millimeter between them. Of how easy it would be to bury his hands in the soft luxury of her hair and breathe in her scent, to lay her across the desk and finish what they'd started at the hotel in South Carolina.

Reaching up, he brushed his hand against the smoothness of her cheek. "Sensuous, lyrical."

She swallowed, her eyes widening as they met his. Then she chuckled dryly. "Oh, yeah, that's me, all right."

Damn straight. "You don't see yourself that way?"

"That's not how women think," she said, pulling away. "It's not like I wake up in the morning all 'goodness, I'm feeling lyrical.'"

He laughed at her tone. "Okay, just the sensual part, then. You do know you're a very beautiful woman?"

She frowned. "What are you, my self-appointed therapist?"

There was that little couch thing beneath the lights, but he didn't want to use it for talking. "Not at all."

"Maybe it's your big-brother instincts run amuck, but—"

"Olivia, nothing I feel toward you is *brotherly*. Or did I not make that clear enough in the hotel elevator?"

Spots of color bloomed in her cheek. "Fair point. But th-that was a one-time thing, an aberration."

Whether it was an isolated incident remained to be

seen. "The attraction between us wasn't a fluke. It's there all the time." Like now.

He didn't move toward her, but he didn't have to. The mutual desire was so palpable, he half expected to see it, like shimmering waves of heat off the asphalt in the summer.

She didn't deny it, but she didn't look happy about it, either. "Wanting something doesn't make it good for you."

The moment stretched between them, interrupted only by the phone ringing. He turned to grab the receiver. "Justin Hawthorne...oh, hey, Kate." Damn.

He and the assistant HR manager were having an early dinner tonight. How could he have almost forgotten when the scheduling had been his idea? A quick midweek meal after work seemed a good compromise between hurting her feelings by rejecting her invitation and potentially leading her on with a more formal date.

"Sure, I can be ready then," he told her. "I was just wrapping up."

Even though his instincts told him not to, he stole a glance in Olivia's direction. Her body was rigid. He remembered the way she'd accused him of flirting with the models and Diane, the indignant humiliation in her eyes when they'd stepped off the elevator and there had been Felicia with her robe and welcome smile.

But nothing happened with Felicia. He hadn't been able to fall into the model's bed right after being in Olivia's arms. Nothing would happen with bright-eyed Kate tonight, but it was clear from Olivia's expression that she saw him as a debauched womanizer.

She was already moving toward the doorway as he

hung up the phone. "We can discuss this tomorrow. Forget I came down here."

What she meant was "forget I admitted wanting you." Doubtful. "Olivia—"

She didn't turn, but it was just as well. What could he have said?

Her annoyance seemed to come from believing he led a carefree bachelor's life, playing the field and answering to no one. He could tell her she was dead wrong, explain to her about the last few years and his sisters, but why? The truth was, he wanted exactly the life Olivia assumed he had.

Besides, he couldn't talk about raising Andy and Lisa, not comfortably, anyway. Bryan had once unthinkingly blurted that women would be touched by Justin's story and would be lining up to "comfort" him. But even ignoring the fact that Justin wasn't going to use his parents' death to score, he didn't know how to express the trapped, almost claustrophobic feeling he'd so often experienced. Sometimes he'd caught himself resenting his two younger sisters, before guiltily remembering they'd lost their mother and father, too. No one had asked for the situation. All he could do was make the best of it, and he'd survived those moments where he'd felt imprisoned and unable to breathe by promising himself a completely different lifestyle as soon as it was possible.

That time was now. He should be living it up, not obsessing over a co-worker who sought steady commitment and disapproved of his yearning for something spontaneous and casual. No, telling her she was wrong about him definitely wasn't the answer. He should be out there proving her *right*.

8

OLIVIA SAT at her desk, drumming her fingers against her keyboard and resisting the urge to ask Meg, the best source of office scuttlebutt, if she'd heard anything about Kate and Justin's date last night. Her friend was sitting in one of the visitor's chairs in Olivia's office, her bare feet propped up in the other chair because she'd needed respite from breaking in a new pair of heels.

So far, Meg had only been talking about where they should grab lunch today. *If she knew something, she would have said so already.* Then again, Meg seemed determined to prove Olivia was interested in the photographer, so maybe she was withholding information just to make Olivia ask.

Well, it wasn't going to work.

Olivia glanced from the e-mail she was answering to Meg's discarded shoes. "Another sale only you have the good luck to happen across? They look expensive."

"But *sexy*."

"Sexy is more important than comfortable?"

"They'll be comfy enough once I've worn 'em a few times. We should get you some sexy heels." Meg studied Olivia, her expression considering.

Olivia actually felt pretty fashionable today. She

liked the red color of her suit and the funky block cut of the jacket.

"And some new clothes to go with the new shoes," Meg pronounced.

Pop. That would be the sound of Olivia's bubble bursting. "What? This is in style. Stormy wore a jacket a lot like mine to an interview last week."

"Yeah, but she wore it over a Sweet Nothings cami-bra, not a blouse buttoned to her chin."

"Oh, sure, diss the suit," Olivia grumbled. "At least I'm not the one with sore feet and potential blisters." Meg was crazy if she thought Olivia, with her recently doubled rent, was going to buy high heels. As if she needed the extra height.

"Assuming I'm not crippled by blisters, you want to do something this weekend?" Meg asked suddenly.

Olivia looked away from her computer again with a sigh. She wasn't getting anything done, but there was a better than even chance that if Meg wasn't here, Olivia would be obsessing about Justin, anyway. "You want me to see what movies are playing?"

"No, let's do something fun. Go somewhere we can meet guys!"

"I don't—"

"All right, let's go somewhere *I* can meet a guy, and you can let me know if you approve of him or not."

"Because I've been known to have such great taste." Olivia laughed. "Okay, sure, why not? Hanging out with you is never boring."

"Cool. We could invite Jeanie, but I'm sure she and Albert have plans. I fully expect them to get engaged any day now."

"At least someone's having good luck with men," Olivia said, unpleasantly aware of how wistful she sounded.

"Hey, Jeanie says you won't let her set you up with Albert's brother. He's a doctor, you know. And cute—I've seen a picture."

But can he kiss? And did he have sexy green eyes that looked at a woman as though he could see all her secret desires? "If you're interested, Meg, you should have Jeanie set *you* up with him."

Meg snorted. "I tried. She told me I might be 'too much' for the reserved doctor. He's probably more your type, anyway."

Olivia tried not to let it bother her that her best friend had twice implied she was boring.

"The fashion show gala is next Friday," Meg said. "You have a date for that?"

"I don't mind going alone. It's more work than anything else. What about you?"

"I have a list of potentials, but I haven't whittled it down yet."

"Hey," Olivia said very casually, as though she'd just happened to think of it, "speaking of dates, didn't Kate—"

"Ha! Jeanie owes me ten bucks." Meg smirked. "I wondered when you were going to get around to asking me what I knew about—"

"Justin!" Olivia signaled wildly with her eyes, hoping Meg would shut up and look behind her, to the sexy blond photographer who had suddenly appeared in the doorway.

"'Morning, ladies." His deep voice made Olivia's body tingle with anticipation.

"Speak of the devil," she muttered.

He folded his arms over his chest. "You didn't by any chance just tell me to go to the devil?"

Despite his inopportune timing, she chuckled. "No, that's not what I said."

"Oh, good. Can I come in? Seeing as how your office has chairs and everything," he kidded.

It was her bad luck that he made her feel like smiling. She liked to think she could withstand his good looks alone, but the total package was harder to resist.

"I guess it would help if I wasn't taking up both the chairs." Meg slid her feet to the floor and bent to retrieve her strappy new shoes.

Justin nodded approvingly toward the heels. "Sexy."

"Thanks." Meg shot a brief I-told-you-so look in Olivia's direction as she stood. "I should be getting back to my job before someone realizes how utterly dispensable I am. See you at lunch, Olivia."

Olivia's so-called friend not only abandoned her, she shut the door when she left.

Justin sat in the chair Meg had vacated. "I should apologize for interrupting, but the truth is, I'm glad to have you alone."

Her pulse jumped. "Actually, I was in the middle of—"

"We never did talk about those sketches yesterday. And I wanted to explain about Kate."

How much had he overheard? "You don't owe me any explanation."

No, Justin supposed he didn't, but after the way she'd looked at him yesterday... It was bothering him not to clear up any misconceptions she had, at least about this. The assistant HR manager was definitely past twenty-one, but she had an innocence that made the idea of his dating her seem too predatory.

"It doesn't matter to me who you ask out," Olivia added, her tone almost lofty, despite the skittish way she wouldn't meet his gaze.

"*She* asked *me*."

For a split second, Olivia's posture sagged, indicating relief, but then she shrugged. "Doesn't really make a difference. It's none of my business, either way."

Her feigned indifference might have really irritated him, if she weren't such a lousy actress.

He leaned forward with his arms across his knees. "I trust you won't repeat this, but I accepted her invitation mainly because I didn't want to hurt her. We had a pleasant dinner and when she told me about some of her interests, I mentioned that there's a guy in accounting who has a lot of the same hobbies."

At the end of the evening, he'd been relieved when Kate had not only acknowledged their lack of chemistry, but had seemed philosophical about the discovery.

As for chemistry...he stared hard into Olivia's eyes. "You seemed troubled when you left the studio yesterday, so I just wanted to let you know that Kate isn't my type."

She looked down, shuffling papers on her desk. "You know who might be? Diane, Steve's assistant. She seems interested."

No kidding—like he'd somehow missed the subtle signs? "Sorry. Can't say I'm drawn to her, either."

"What about blondes?"

"I beg your pardon?" The only woman he was currently entranced with was the one with jet-black hair that fell in waves over her left shoulder, past the swell of her breast. Of course, he saw the swell only in his mind's eye. Her shapeless jacket camouflaged the curves Justin had committed to memory.

"You weren't interested in a brunette or redhead, so I thought maybe a—a blonde."

Too bad one of his sisters wasn't here to translate Femalese. He honestly couldn't tell if Olivia wanted the buffer of his hooking up with the next gorgeous blonde who crossed his path, or if she wanted assurance that he wouldn't. Did *she* even know what she wanted?

A brief scorching memory of her kisses made him reconsider. Oh yeah, she knew what she wanted. She just wasn't going for it.

"Well, thanks for the suggestions," he said sarcastically. "But I think I can figure out my love life all by myself. I'm not even afraid to admit when I want someone."

Her eyes flashed at him. "I'm not afraid, I'm sensible. Kissing you was not sensible."

"It was hot."

"Men," she muttered. "Yes, it was hot. But, so what? What exactly do you want from me, Justin? Companionship, and long talks at the end of the day, knowing that there's someone there for you in the years to come—or sex?"

He blinked, startled by the angrily voiced question.

Frankly, coming from her, the companionship part sounded better than he'd expected it to. Talking to Olivia was certainly never boring, and on the drive back to Atlanta, he'd enjoyed their conversation. It was the "years to come" part he instinctively shied away from. He was more on the day-to-day plan.

After a moment of taut silence, Olivia exhaled a soft, frustrated sigh. "Yeah. That's what I thought.

"WAIT UNTIL you see Lindi's sister," Bryan said gleefully. "She's almost as gorgeous as Lindi herself, and that's saying something. Or, maybe we could find you a nice homely gal?"

Justin started, mentally replaying the last few minutes to try to figure out what they'd been discussing. "Sorry. What?"

Bryan leaned back against the vinyl padded bench on the other side of the booth. "I don't get it. You're the one who asked me if I knew someone single. You change your mind?"

Specifically, Justin had asked to meet someone attractive and fun. He'd known Bryan had the numbers of half a dozen women who fit that bill. Of course, Justin didn't want to go out with one of his friend's exes, so the sister of Bryan's current flame had been ideal.

"No, I'm looking forward to this," Justin said. "Thanks. In fact, I was watching the door, seeing if the girls were here yet."

Bryan followed his friend's gaze to the front of Hewitt's, which was doing big Saturday night business. "You're watching for Lindi and Hope?"

"Yeah."

"Two women you've never actually seen before? Right. You wanna tell me what's really going on, pal?"

Not especially. Justin had felt on edge ever since his confrontation with Olivia on Thursday. They'd managed to put it aside long enough to talk about Miss Peach's—the Southern bed-and-breakfast they'd be shooting at next week—but he couldn't shake his exasperation. Olivia had worked her way under his skin like a splinter.

Even though she had a point, part of one, anyway, he resented the way she said he'd be no good for her. He'd never deliberately hurt anyone, and how could he possibly be any worse for her than that cheating ex? *Let it go.* He didn't want a relationship, and even if she were willing to have a fling, she'd probably be very prim and proper and buttoned-up about it.

In his mind, he heard elevator music and smelled the tang of the ocean on Olivia's skin as he kissed her. Okay, fine, she'd be hot and wild and glorious in his bed—a nonissue if she didn't want to be there.

"There they are." Bryan pointed toward two lithe young women, one with curly strawberry-blond hair, the other with shorter, darker red-gold hair. "The one on the left is Hope. I know you're a little rusty at this, but she'll love you—and I mean that in the free-spirited unmatrimonial way. Have some fun."

"I plan to." Because despite what a certain co-worker might think, there was nothing wrong with a little fun.

"MEGAN NICOLE JANSEN!" Olivia picked her drink up off the bar, and turned to her friend. "I want your word that you didn't know he was going to be here. Is this why you insisted on the skirt?"

Ducking her head, Meg sipped her margarita, either stalling or counting on the tequila for confessional courage. Possibly both.

"I can't believe you did this." Olivia felt even more self-conscious than she had when she'd stepped inside the informal nightclub.

Although she knew other women were dressed in far flashier outfits than her black skirt and formfitting cranberry-colored top, she felt exposed. She'd hoped the round of drinks she and Meg had ordered would loosen her up enough to check out the small dance floor, as Meg had wanted to do. But spotting Justin among a foursome at the pool tables destroyed any chances of her relaxing in the near future.

Somehow she doubted that the petite redhead who clung to his biceps and giggled up at him whenever she missed her shots was his other sister.

"Now, don't overreact," Meg said. "I told Justin I wanted to go someplace new and asked what places he thought were fun."

"And he didn't mention that he'd be at this particular one on Saturday night?"

"Well...it might have come up. Look, if you're really as uninterested in the man as you claim, why does it matter that he's here?"

Oh, no, you don't. "That is not the point, Meg."

Her friend swiveled idly back and forth on her bar stool. "As for why I badgered you into wearing the skirt, it's because you have nice legs. Show them off. If not for yourself, then for all of us who don't have great gams," Meg said with exaggerated self-pity.

"Laying it on a little thick, aren't you?" Olivia didn't want to be amused, but it was hard to stay mad. Truth be told, Meg would be a much better match for the outgoing photographer, Justin, than Olivia would ever be. Inside, she was still too much the shy wallflower.

"Forgive me?" Meg pressed. "He said he'd be here with a friend of his, and I just wanted him to see how good you could look outside the office. But regardless of my intentions, I shouldn't have interfered." Meg sighed. "Do you want to leave?"

Going elsewhere would only demonstrate that she was letting herself care too much about Justin and what happened in his personal life. "We can stay...but you're paying for the next round."

"Deal. Now, help me look for hot guys."

Olivia cast a halfhearted glance around the room, but her gaze strayed back to Justin, chatting with two gorgeous women in tight clothes she'd never be comfortable wearing and a dark-haired man who gave Justin a run for the money in the looks department. The single adult version of the cool clique. Olivia remembered the parties she'd attended with Sean, feeling uneasily frumpy next to the models and stylists he'd flirted with. The times she'd deliberately picked sexier clothes, she'd spent the evening fussing with her hem and neckline.

If Meg hadn't dragged her out tonight, Olivia would have been content to stay in and watch DVDs. Every night she'd spent at home in her teenage years with her nose buried in novels or watching her mom's old romantic movies, she'd wanted to be out living it up, but as an adult who'd had that chance, she'd decided it wasn't all she'd cracked it up to be.

Then again, her expectations had been far more naive than realistic. Her mom had assured her she'd blossom into a swan and meet her prince, and Olivia's equally well-meaning dad had told her boys would one day recognize her beauty. She'd moved away from home with storybook hopes that had left her heart vulnerable.

Time to get real.

On Monday, she would tell Jeanie to have Albert's brother call—forget the palate-cleansing man-fast and step up the dating diet. If she didn't find a healthy relationship that wouldn't add on pounds of emotional baggage, she might succumb to something dangerously decadent she'd regret later. She kept saying she would develop some discipline when it came to men and find a nourishing salad kind of guy, but then she spent all her time fantasizing about the dessert tray.

Meg nudged her. "You okay?"

"Never better. Time for those drinks."

"Sure. After that, you want to check out the action on the dance floor?"

Olivia forbade herself to look toward—*Justin*—the pool tables again. "Any chance I could interest you in a quick game of darts first?" For some reason she really felt the need to throw something.

JUSTIN KNEW a lot of men didn't enjoy dancing, and he'd always thought those guys were missing out on a prime opportunity to get close to women. Take now, for instance. Hope was a sexy and vivacious date, and the way she gyrated on the dance floor in time to the pop song the DJ had selected held a lot of promise for the rest of the evening. But his very male appreciation of her attributes was marred by a certain co-worker who shouldn't be here.

"Is there something wrong?" Lindi's sister asked, her chipper voice making him even more exasperated with himself. Why wasn't *he* feeling chipper?

"Not at all. I'm having a great time." He smiled widely for effect and absently moved his body to the beat.

He'd been shocked to see Olivia and Meg throwing darts in the corner of his favorite bar—even more shocked at the sight of Olivia's long legs beneath the hem of a flirty skirt—but quickly realized he'd done this to himself when he'd answered Meg's seemingly innocent questions about his plans for the weekend. Olivia had made it clear nothing was going to happen between them, and Justin wasn't going to let her presence here spoil his good time. He'd vowed to forget she was even in the building.

Which would be easier to accomplish if Meg hadn't taken to the dance floor with some 80s throwback, leaving Olivia to tell the same guy three times now she didn't want a drink. At least, that's what Justin had deduced was happening from over the top of Hope's head. Olivia looked increasingly tense, and the man she'd shaken her head at was leaning closer than personal-space etiquette allowed.

"Hope, would you mind if I excused myself for a minute? I see a friend of mine from work, and she looks like she could use a hand." He told himself that Hope presented exactly the kind of opportunity he'd been looking forward to and that it was stupid to walk away, but if Olivia needed him...

"Sure, why not?" She didn't seem to mind at all, and he mentally kicked himself. What were the odds another easygoing, beautiful woman would just fall into his lap?

Sparing a second to mourn the loss of the uncomplicated, stress-relieving fling they might have had, Justin strode off the dance floor. As he neared Olivia, the would-be suitor who had been bothering her stomped off, his expression enraged. Olivia, watching the man's retreat, noticed Justin, and her gray eyes widened.

He moved toward her, trying to ignore how stunning she looked tonight. "Hi."

"Hi." She swallowed. "Small world."

He raised an eyebrow. "You mean because of the remarkable coincidence that days after mentioning to your friend that I'd be here, here you are?"

"It was not my idea."

"Trust me, I didn't think it was." He sat on the stool next to her. "Although that would have been extremely flattering."

"If your ego needs to be stroked, find someone else."

And if his ego wasn't what needed stroking? "What happened to the Romeo wanna-be?"

She tilted her head, appraising him. "You were watching me?"

"I was on my way to the bar and noticed you over here. I was coming to say hi when the guy almost mowed me down."

"Really?"

"No, not really. I've been stealing glances this way for the past ten minutes, wondering when Meg was going to get back here and rescue you."

Olivia laughed. "Meg's having fun, and I don't need rescuing. When the guy stuck his hand under my skirt, I told him I'd knee him in the groin if I didn't think what he had there was too small to rack."

"You said what? Never mind, I got it the first time." If he weren't silently applauding her, he might have winced in masculine empathy. "Not that I'm unimpressed, but be careful antagonizing guys who've been drinking."

"No worries on that score." She jerked a thumb over her shoulder. "There's a bouncer hovering right behind me. I think he was watching for a signal that I needed help."

"Oh." Having charged over here like an overzealous white knight on his trusty steed, Justin felt a bit silly.

"Won't your date be wondering what's taking you so long?" Olivia asked.

"My date?"

"Cute redhead with the erotic dance moves."

He echoed her earlier question. "You've been watching me?"

Her delicate skin flushed, and she lifted her drink from the railing. "I might have glanced your direction once or twice."

They lapsed into silence, and Justin stared out at the colorful crowd of people dancing. Hope was gyrating in front of a brawny man with a crew cut who seemed to be appreciating her attention more than Justin had.

"Better get back out there before you're permanently replaced," Olivia said, following his gaze.

"It's all right," he told her. "We didn't exactly click."

Olivia shook her head in reproach. "I told you, you should find yourself a blonde. I hear they have more fun."

Studying the dark ponytail that brushed past the nape of her neck, he almost asked her when she was going to let herself have fun. Why was she here on the sideline while her friend was out enjoying herself? Olivia's soft clingy long-sleeved shirt and sexy skirt were a good start, but her expression said she'd rather be hiding behind a book or pair of baggy jeans.

He wanted to tell her how amazing she looked, how aroused he got just watching her smile, but he stopped himself. He'd flirted, he'd kissed her, he'd bluntly addressed the attraction between them, but it had gotten him nowhere. As someone with two sisters—as someone who'd stalked over to liberate Olivia from unwanted male attention—Justin respected women too much to push. He didn't need Olivia threatening to rack him, too.

"You know what," he conceded, "you may be on to something."

Her mouth fell open, his easy agreement obviously startling her.

"No more flirting with you." He grinned. "Okay, even I didn't buy that. But I do get the message. I'll forget we ever kissed. Forget about trying to kiss you again, put an end to all that wicked wondering about what it would feel like to make love to you, to feel you around me."

In the deep V of her uncharacteristically low neckline, her skin took on a rosy glow. Her eyes were smoky with answering speculation about what they'd be like together. He bit back a grin; she didn't look so convinced that retreat was what she wanted.

He tried to remember the models he'd heard her mention in conjunction with the B and B shoot. Wasn't one of them a Victoria? No, Veronica. Veronica and Toni. "Any chance Veronica or Toni is a blonde?"

A barely audible squeak escaped her, the sound soft but indignant. Despite his respecting her wishes, Olivia was clearly affronted that he'd go from mentioning making love with her to asking for an introduction to a potential lover. Ah, jealousy. The one tack he hadn't tried. Instead of assuring her nothing had happened between him and Kate, and telling her that he and Hope hadn't hit it off, maybe he should have encouraged her to think whatever she wanted.

And I'm back in the game. "Maybe you could put in a good word for me."

She surprised him with a smooth, almost smug, smile. "As a matter of fact, Tony *is* a blonde, and I'd be happy to put in a good word." *Take that,* her eyes said.

All right, so jealousy hadn't done the trick, either. He looked back out on to the dance floor, where his date and her new friend were cuddled together as though a slow song was being played instead of a hip-hop remix. He had to do something—and soon—to convince Olivia to act on the desire he knew she felt, or put aside his own desire for her once and for all.

Because, right now, the woman was single-handedly ruining his love life.

9

THE SCENE that greeted Olivia as she slid her sunglasses up onto her head and stepped inside was an odd one. The antebellum bed-and-breakfast had been invaded, but not by the Union army this time. Models were sprawled across the sitting room, studying each other's portfolios and loudly exchanging industry gossip over music coming from a portable CD player. The rock sound of Nickelback was a bizarre contrast to the antique furniture and gleaming hardwood floor.

Most B and Bs didn't do a thriving business midweek, outside of summer or major holiday seasons. People preferred to take romantic getaways on long weekends, when they could sleep in with their lover the next morning, and the proprietors of Miss Peach's were always happy to pick up a little extra revenue by letting Sweet Nothings use some space during slow times.

Rick and another stylist were lining up the order of who needed to report for hair and makeup. A representative from a local catering service was handing out bottles of water and trying to figure out where to set up the light-fare buffet for crew members and the models, should they actually eat. But Olivia didn't have to look twice to know that Justin wasn't among the throng.

If he'd been here, her body would already be vibrat-

ing like a tuning fork. Despite being sensible enough to
arrange a blind date with Albert's brother for this coming Saturday, she couldn't reason with her libido. She
should have been relieved by Justin's declaration Saturday night to move on, with no further attempts to seduce her. Instead, she'd become even more preoccupied than before.

Justin was probably upstairs, scoping out the lay of
the land with his assistant, Dan, an intern from one of
the local colleges. Most of the "couples" shots would
take place in Miss Peach's honeymoon suite, a room
big enough for the portable lights, complete with a lux-
urious bathroom with a whirlpool tub and a private
balcony overlooking the duck pond. Furniture could
be altered slightly and bed linens switched to give the
same room several different looks.

The balcony would be a great location…to say nothing of the four-poster bed.

Olivia hesitated at the possibility of going up the
curved staircase and finding herself alone with Justin
and that bed. A delicious shiver went up her spine, but
was halted somewhere around the eighth vertebrae by
a male voice—the wrong male voice—calling out her
name.

Model Chad Langley stepped away from where he'd
been talking to Veronica Shapiro. Veronica, known to
friends as VJ, wore a pair of Sweet Nothings draw-
string lounging pants and a button-down shirt that
could be removed without smudging her hair and
makeup. Chad, on the other hand, was dressed in
baggy shorts. Models definitely needed to be comfort-

able with their bodies, but Chad had always struck Olivia as just a little too eager to strut around shirtless.

Her silent groan now had nothing to do with the male model's exposed pecs and more to do with his being one of Sean's best pals.

Chad approached, his overly friendly smile a clear attempt to remind Olivia that *he* hadn't been the one who'd slept with her roommate. "Long time, no see, beautiful. I was pumped when the agency said you called and requested me for this."

She returned his smile. "Well, you're perfect for the job."

"Heard you got rid of the loser."

"You heard right." She doubted he sang the same tune when Sean was in earshot.

"You deserve better."

"Thanks. That seems to be the popular opinion." Trying not to be obvious about looking over his shoulder rather than making eye contact, she glanced behind him, again studying the staircase in anticipation of Justin's possible arrival.

It was understandable that she'd be anxious about his whereabouts—this was a photo shoot, and he was the photographer. Her interest was strictly sexual.

"*Professional,*" she blurted. "I meant professional."

"Excuse me?" Chad's dark eyebrows lifted, but if he had questions about her mental stability, he didn't let them slow him down. "Hey, Olivia, since you're unattached now, I was thinking maybe we could have dinner at the end of the day. I always liked you."

It would have been a more flattering invitation if it hadn't been aimed in the vicinity of her chest. She suspected what he'd really "always liked" was her 36D bra size.

Tempted to respond, "Yoo-hoo! I'm up here," she instead went with, "Sorry. I have plans."

He didn't need to know they consisted of washing her hair and going to bed early.

Ending the conversation before he could ask for details or suggest another time, Olivia turned away and nodded hello to VJ. The striking brunette would be the lead model for this issue and would help launch a new line of lacy teddies. Olivia, Meg, Justin and Steve had picked out the colors they thought would photograph best on her, but Olivia wanted to double-check the bedroom décor and confirm the choices with the wardrobe mistress.

They'd be starting soon and even though Justin had storyboard mock-ups to go by, she was supposed to be supervising here. She needed to stop stalling. Raising her eyes to the staircase, she sucked in a sharp breath when Justin's gaze met hers from the landing. The buzz of those around her and the voice of the lead singer of Nickelback faded into silence as she experienced a total *Gone With the Wind* moment.

It was too easy, too appealing, to imagine Justin coming to claim her, sweeping her up into a passionate embrace and carrying her to that four-poster bed. She blinked. If Rhett and Scarlett were done commandeering her thoughts, it was time to get to work. She made her way up the steps, joining Justin on the landing that overlooked the crowded great room, with its fireplace and occupied love seats.

"I figured you were up here," she said. "All set to go in the bedroom?"

"Absolutely." His wolfish grin made her a little light-headed. "I'm ready whenever you are."

"Great," she countered with a cool smile. "Just wanted to make sure nothing's wrong with your equipment."

He chuckled grudgingly. "C'mon, Dan can round up the first two models while you give me your input. That is, if you're finished putting me in my place?"

Her grin turned impish. "For now, anyway."

Her mood was unpredictably cheeky today. Come to think of it, she'd been feeling a little different ever since seeing Justin Saturday night. They both knew he'd abandoned his date—who had *sure thing* written all over her—because he'd been worried about Olivia. If Sean had been dancing with an alluring woman so clearly moving in an imitation of sex, he wouldn't have noticed the building burning down, much less someone trapped in an awkward situation.

The funny thing was, despite Justin's chivalry, Olivia honestly hadn't needed rescue. In the past, a man who'd hit on her so relentlessly, his eyes leering and his hand wandering, would have left her feeling shaky and vulnerable. This time, she'd had no desire to hide in a dark corner, folding her arms to disguise her cleavage. She'd simply told the guy where to stick it, and later, even enjoyed herself for a little while out on the dance floor with Meg.

Go, me.

Olivia walked into the bedroom suite and asked the waiting assistant to send up VJ and Tony, then she followed Justin out onto the stone balcony, where he asked her opinion about possible poses. With that taken care of, she cleared her throat, realizing there was something she should probably address. She'd told Justin to take his sexual interest somewhere else, yet when he'd promised to do exactly that, he'd caught her so off guard she'd childishly allowed herself a moment of fun at his expense. She should resolve any confusion she'd caused before the shoot proceeded.

"Justin, I have a confession to make."

"Sounds serious." He stood at the camera he'd placed on a tripod just outside the French doors, fiddling with settings.

"Well, it's about Tony—"

"The blonde?" Justin grinned, looking so chipper about the prospect of meeting the model that Olivia briefly considered shoving him into the rippling duck pond below.

Stop being jealous, he's only doing what you *asked.* Dammit. "Yes. The blonde."

"Great. I've been looking forward to meeting her."

"Justin, Tony's not exactly your type. You see—"

"Wait a second." When he glanced up, his smile had vanished. "Enough with the mixed signals. My love life is none of your business."

"True, but—"

"There are no 'buts' here, Olivia. I tolerated your very transparent disapproval of my going out with Kate, but this is becoming a pattern for you. Is Toni married?"

"Well, no."

"Then, drop the subject. I'm a grown man, with a

man's desires, and I won't apologize for having a healthy sex drive."

"You're not listening."

"No, *you* aren't. You're free to turn me down if that's really what you want, sweetheart, but you can't decide who I date."

"But—"

"So, regardless of whether or not you approve, if I want to ask Toni out, I will."

"You tell her, handsome."

Oh, no. Olivia jerked her head around and spotted Tony Wainwright, a six foot blond man who had abs like corrugated steel. He'd also had more boyfriends in the last year than she'd had her whole life.

Tony clucked his tongue. "Honestly, Livvy, darling, I thought you'd have more respect for people's personal preferences."

Olivia didn't have to look at Justin to know he'd swung his gaze back to her.

He spoke through clenched teeth, so softly she could barely hear him. "Is that Toni? Toni, the blond model?"

"Y-yes." Taking tiny imperceptible steps, she edged away from the balcony back toward the carpeted bedroom, knowing she'd be lucky if Justin didn't throw *her* to the ducks. "I never lied, you know. He is blond, and he is a model."

"Are we getting started, or not?" a female voice asked. VJ stood in the doorway in a rose-colored satin teddy. "'Cause, no offense to the designers of these things, but if I've got time to kill, I'm changing into something more comfy."

"We're definitely getting started." Justin's bright smile was like unexpected sunshine in the middle of a thunderstorm. Clearly, a beautiful woman in pink lacy underthings was all he needed to bring him out of a bad mood.

He walked toward the two models, extending a hand. "We haven't had the chance to meet yet. I'm—"

"Divine," Tony pronounced, reaching over to shake the photographer's hand. "Justin, right?"

"Er...yeah." Justin nodded, his manner friendly and professional despite the I'm-going-to-get-you-for-this glare he discreetly sent Olivia.

After exchanging introductions with VJ, Justin directed Dan on where to position the lights. The first round of shots were of VJ alone, sitting at the small corner vanity in a short filmy robe that matched her lingerie. Justin got some photographs from behind her, capturing her reflection in the mirror. Then there was one of her on the balcony, with Tony standing beside her, wearing one of the men's robes on sale for Father's Day.

When VJ went into the suite's bathroom to don her second wardrobe selection, the male model approached Justin. "So, tell me about yourself. Heard you were with Hilliard before this?"

"That's right." Justin smiled weakly. "Er, Tony, I feel I should...if you overheard anything earlier that.... Excuse me, I need to talk to Olivia."

Then he stalked across the bedroom to where Olivia sat on the vanity stool.

"I've decided that these are aptly named," he told her.

"What are?"

"Shoots." He hissed the word under his breath. "I feel like I could shoot *you*. I think he was going to ask me out."

She bit her bottom lip, but at the last second, a small laugh escaped.

His eyes narrowed. "Was that a giggle?"

Definitely. "Of course not. Look, I'm sorry. I didn't set out to put you in an awkward position with Tony."

He leaned down so that his face was level with hers. "Don't use the word *position*. Right now, the mental pictures are just too scary."

His expression was so comically stricken, that this time, her laugh tumbled out freely, leaving her with the exhilarated feeling of not holding anything back.

Justin's gaze lingered on her mouth, and heat stole through her. She swayed slightly toward him, moving as easily and unconsciously as a reed in the wind. The sensation of her body having its own will was liberating. For one heady second, she fantasized turning herself over to his will.

"You have a very sexy laugh," he told her.

No one had ever said that before, and she couldn't say whether she was more affected by his words or his husky, intimate tone.

Trying to stem the wave of desire she felt, she joked away the compliment. "Isn't that the kind of thing a man says because it sounds better than 'you have nice breasts'?"

"No." He lowered his voice to a whisper she strained to hear. "I say you have a sexy laugh because it's so uninhibited and bold, all I can think about is what an incredible lover you must be. When I hear you laugh like that, Olivia, I want to be inside you. But, since you mention it, your breasts are incredible, too."

She expected his gaze to drop to her chest, but it didn't. Instead, his eyes held hers, seducing her with their intensity and his frank arousal. She fidgeted in her seat, dampness pooling between her legs as her entire body responded to what he'd said. Her skin felt fevered, and her nipples had grown taut, almost begging for his notice.

Self-preservation demanded she get back to the original topic, though her suddenly dry mouth made speaking difficult. "Um...if there's anything I can do to smooth over the Tony problem, I'm there."

"You could start by helping me get rid of any traumatic mental images. I need something else to picture in my mind."

The man had the clearest green eyes she'd ever seen. "Like something soothing, you mean?"

His gaze left her face briefly, glancing sidelong toward the decadent piece of furniture that dominated the room. "Not exactly."

She felt her chest rise as she sucked in a breath and knew that the motion beneath the square neckline of her knit top caught his attention.

"Where did you want me? On the bed?"

Olivia and Justin both started, and she peered around him to find VJ, her expression benign as she brushed a microscopic piece of lint from the dark blue crushed velvet teddy she wore. When Justin turned back to his work, Olivia couldn't help feeling briefly jealous of the woman who now held his focus. Though

Olivia's long-sleeved top was in fashion and her camel-colored slacks hugged her hips, she wished she'd worn something sexier.

Seduce him in silk, mesmerize him in mesh.... Some people had little devils on their shoulders, she had rogue ad copy writers.

Soon it was time to switch couples, bringing in Stormy and Chad. Since the corporate belief at Sweet Nothings was that it helped foster romantic lingerie-buying feelings in the primarily female subscribers, couples worked in exclusive pairs for each issue. There would be no pictures of Stormy with Tony, or VJ with Chad. Men who picked up the catalog probably wouldn't notice, but women might be unconsciously sensitive to such a detail.

Olivia was glad to see Tony go before Justin had any more reason to be annoyed with the misunderstanding she'd created, but she wasn't thrilled about Chad coming in to replace the other man. He strode into the room wearing a pair of red silk boxers.

She blinked. "You're supposed to have the dark blue or black shorts, Chad."

"I thought red was more eye-catching." The man grinned at her, one eyebrow raised. "Don't you think so, Liv?"

Her recently boosted self-confidence laced her voice. "What I think is that bright red clashes completely with the cranberry accents we're using and that you should use the wardrobe choices we pay you to use. Now go change."

Chad's handsome face got a little less handsome with his surly scowl. "You should think about getting another boyfriend. I don't remember you being this cranky when you were with Sean."

"And I don't remember her asking your opinion," Justin said softly. His tone was casual, but something in the expression Olivia couldn't see from where she stood made Chad swallow nervously.

"I'm just gonna find those dark blue boxers," the model said, stepping aside to make way for Stormy to enter the room.

The gorgeous young woman wore one of the shoot's sexier selections. A hunter-green floral lace babydoll slip hugged her slender body, emphasizing her curvier areas. The halter-top style left plenty of creamy cleavage, but the floral pattern swirling over the sheer mesh covered enough that they wouldn't have to airbrush out any nipple exposure. Seeing the appreciative way Justin watched the model, Olivia suddenly hated her job.

She wanted to be the one dressed in provocative lingerie for him—without the four other people present, of course. Funny when she thought about it, because even with her employee discount, she couldn't recall wearing much lingerie for any boyfriend. That wasn't to say she stuck to plain white cotton, she'd just never bought clothing for the express purpose of being naked later. She recalled the way Justin had kissed her in the elevator, the way he'd made her feel as if no one else even existed, as if he was lost in her. To be the focus of such sensual concentration again, she couldn't think of anything in the Sweet Nothings catalog she wouldn't wear.

Chad returned quickly, wearing black silk boxers

and a hangdog expression. "Sorry about earlier, Liv. I really just thought the red would photograph well."

"Forgiven and forgotten," she said absently.

Her attention was on Justin and the denim snug across his backside as he bent over to turn down the comforter and give the bed a more rumpled look for the photos. His T-shirt was short-sleeved, and Olivia stared in unabashed appreciation at his well-muscled arms.

"Maybe I could make it up to you with dinner?" Chad was saying.

She almost rolled her eyes. If he thought he could use his earlier attitude to get a date with her, he was sadly mistaken. "I told you already—"

"It doesn't have to be tonight, since you have plans."

Justin straightened and glanced Olivia's way. His gaze was questioning, openly curious about her supposed plans.

"So are you seeing someone, or is it a casual thing?"

"Hmm?" It took Olivia a second to realize Chad was asking about her nonexistent date. She wasn't good at dishonesty, and nothing came to mind.

Before she knew it, Justin had crossed the room toward her. He threw his arm across her shoulder and faced down Chad. "It's not casual enough that we see other people."

What?

Chad reverted to scowling, and slunk away.

"What was that about?" Olivia muttered to her loose-cannon photographer.

"I figure if our 'date' gets back to Tony, it'll clear my

good name, so to speak. You did say you were willing to help."

"Oh." That made sense.

Dismissing the subject, he looked away from her and smiled at Stormy. "Always a pleasure to see you. Could we get a stylist to play with your bangs just a bit, though? Need to see more of that lovely face."

The model's hair was styled in an old-fashioned sexy fall across her forehead, almost covering one eye. Olivia and Justin wanted to keep the bedroom effect without obscuring her features, so everyone waited as the stylist finished his work and added another hair-spray-scented layer to the room.

Justin reloaded film and snapped his camera closed. "Okay, this set was supposed to be a little steamier, right?"

The lights were carefully adjusted, dimmed to suggest intimacy but not so much that the view of the all-important merchandise was compromised. Chad and Stormy sat at the top of the bed, amid cranberry-colored pillows, the dark colors they both wore contrasting nicely with the creamy sheets.

The sheets weren't actually satin, but they looked smooth and expensive, and Olivia could almost feel them sliding against her heated skin. She should go downstairs to get some air, but, irrationally, she didn't want to leave Justin with Stormy.

Because Chad, Dan and the on-call stylist perched on the edge of the bathroom counter aren't enough to chaperone?

This was crazy. She worked around lingerie for a living and had even attended fashion show parties where some of the models mingled among guests wearing little more than slips. But today was different. In some indefinable way, Olivia felt as if she was waking from a sort of sexual hibernation, more alert than ever before.

Justin frowned. "I need you to move your arm up a little more," he directed Chad.

The male model sat behind Stormy, holding her with one beefy arm around her midsection, careful not to obscure the intricate design of the ribboned halter top. Plus, if he used the shoot to grope Stormy, she'd use her brown belt in karate to kick his butt.

Instead of taking a picture, Justin shook his head. "That's still not quite right. Looks posed."

"It *is* posed," Chad grumbled.

"Try this instead," Justin said. "No arms around her. Lean forward and plant one hand on the bed next to her...on her right. On the left, just lay your hand against her leg." Stormy was sitting with her legs tucked loosely against her, and Chad slid a hand just above her knee.

"Better," Justin praised. "We've got an unobstructed view of the product now. Stormy, tilt your head to the side. And you, turn like you're going to kiss her neck."

Chad only partially angled his head in that direction, then paused, waiting for the pictures. Olivia could tell he wasn't excited about any photographs where his face wouldn't be clearly visible.

At Justin's sigh of impatience, Olivia stood, ready to give instructions to the male model, but Justin spoke before she could. "Watch me."

Why he was walking toward her?

"Look, Chad, this is what I want from you, okay?" Justin was talking to the clueless male model, but he looked at Olivia while he spoke. "This needs to be hot. Sexy. This picture is about wanting a woman. Making women feel desirable. It's about arousal."

Arousal. That certainly covered why her palms, and other places, were suddenly damp.

Justin put a hand on her shoulder and spun her around so her back bumped his chest. He brushed her hair aside, the strands tickling the sensitive flesh of her neck as he bent his head toward her. His breath was a warm, ethereal caress on her skin, and his mouth hovered millimeters away. She arched toward him, the imagined feel of his lips against her almost tangible.

Justin stepped away abruptly, and for a moment, no one spoke. "You, uh, get the idea, right, Chad? Forget whether or not I'm getting your best side."

Clenching her hands into fists to stop the way her fingers were shaking, Olivia stared sightlessly at the couple on the bed. Did they know she'd forgotten their existence when Justin's mouth had almost but not quite grazed her skin? Could anyone—could *he*—possibly know she was tingling with awareness, wet and swollen from wanting him? Her legs threatened to sag beneath her, but she couldn't make her muscles function well enough to return to the seat she'd had earlier.

When Justin began taking pictures again, she reminded herself to breathe. *I have to do something.* Any more of his verbal instructions to the couple on the bed about how to touch—or worse, live demonstrations— would send her over the edge.

"New plan," she announced, hoping no one else could hear the desperate edge in her voice.

Justin darted a quizzical glance her way, gesturing

toward Stormy and Chad. "This isn't what we talked about?"

"No, it is. I just had a, um, brainstorm." Anxiety attack, was more like it. "This is about...." Sex. And the fact that she suddenly wanted it. Badly.

"About?" he prompted.

She really needed to get a hold of herself—or him. "About the product, the lingerie. So let's bring it more into focus. Stormy, how are you pedicurewise?"

Justin lifted an eyebrow. "We going for a foot fetish shot?"

Olivia ignored him, knowing Stormy was modeling some of their synthetic marabou-trimmed "bedroom pumps" later.

"I was at the salon yesterday." The model pointed her toes and lifted her foot off the mattress a few inches, showing a shapely ankle and coral-painted nails.

"Perfect." Olivia quickly outlined her suggestion that Stormy go change out of the featured babydoll slip and into anything else that left her bare from the knees down.

Minutes later, Stormy and Chad were reclining on the bed, their legs loosely entangled. Stormy's painted toes and the models' naked calves would be in soft focus toward the foot of the bed. The real picture would be the babydoll slip artfully draped over an antique wooden stand probably used for guest towels. Chad's feet turned out to be easier to work with than the arrogant model himself, and the planned effect would be that the discarded garment was responsible for what was happening in the bed. Olivia was just thankful the new shot didn't require such detailed orchestrations of how the couple should pose.

The day was long, but the rest of the shoot went smoothly. After the models had been sent home, Dan, Olivia and Justin pushed pieces of furniture back to their original places and wrapped up cords for the lights.

Dan glanced at his watch, then at Justin. "Hey, I don't want to bail if you need me, but I have a midterm tomorrow, and—"

"Go. We got it."

"There might still be one or two people packing up," Dan said, "if you need any more help."

Justin looked at Olivia, who shook her head, then back at the college intern. "Nope, we're about done here, too. Study hard, and have a beer for me tomorrow when you're done."

Dan grinned. "Will do."

The intern grabbed his jacket and car keys and left. Olivia was alone with the man she'd been watching, wanting, all day long.

"Bold move," Justin said as he ran a cloth over a camera lens. "That idea you had."

He meant the pictures he'd taken earlier, the ones that would only show the models' feet. The owners of Sweet Nothings had discussed at past meetings that while some companies saved money by photographing the clothes and not using models for their catalogs, buyers purchased lingerie because they were in a very specific mood. A personal mood that was best created when they saw the lingerie on sexy female models that women wanted to emulate and being enjoyed by sexy male models women wanted to impress.

The reminder that she'd gone against company policy made Olivia regret her earlier spontaneity. "We have other pictures if Steve doesn't like the still lifes."

"No, I think yours will be great," Justin said encouragingly. "Want to take a peek at what I got on digital? The pictures will be better after I've had a chance to play with them, but..."

"Sure." The creative spark, the excitement over what they might have produced together, was a good feeling. Nice to experience something other than mind-numbing lust.

He pushed the door shut and picked up one of the digital cameras. When he sat on the bed, patting the mattress next to him with his free hand, the springs groaned suggestively.

Welcome back to our regularly scheduled mind-numbing lust.

She took a seat, kicking off her shoes and tucking her feet under her. Justin hit a silver button on the high-tech camera and sped through some images, including one unflattering shot of Chad that made her rethink how much Sweet Nothings was paying him for the day.

Obviously feeling the same way, Justin scowled. "He may have the right look, but there's furniture in this room that's less wooden. Okay, here. These are the ones we want." He hit another button and handed the camera to her so she could better see the small digitized screen.

He had software back at the office that would allow

him to make all kinds of adjustments, but the raw product was promising. The pictures didn't have the voyeuristic quality of the consumer watching two other people. Instead, it allowed the consumer to imagine she *was* one of the people.

"This is way better than him kissing her neck," she said, thinking aloud.

His eyebrows lifted, and she realized she may have sounded unintentionally derisive about what had been his suggestion.

"N-not that the neck-kissing was bad." On the contrary, Justin's lips feathering over her skin had been amazing. "Just that those shots weren't working."

"I'd have to agree." His gaze locked with hers. "They weren't generating any heat."

Her pulse pounded. "Heat's important."

"Vital."

Muffled footsteps thudded on the landing, and the staircase creaked. The noises were light-years away, though. An entire separate universe was contained in this bedroom.

Justin reached for the camera. His long fingers brushed the delicate skin of her wrist. "Do you really have plans tonight?"

Other than go home and fantasize about him? "No."

"So, you were just trying to get rid of Chad? I have to say, I was a little jealous thinking about another guy being with you." He brushed a hand over her shoulder, pushing her hair back and threading his fingers through it. "Touching you."

With agonizing gentleness, he traced the tip of his

middle finger along her lips, rubbing a slow circle. "Kissing you."

She trembled inside. "Well, there wasn't really anyone I'd be kissing tonight."

"There is now."

10

MAYBE A wiser woman would have stopped to think this over. Olivia, on the other hand, cupped Justin's neck, angled her head and kissed him eagerly. For hours, they'd worked at staging the illusion of passion, and all along the real thing had been burning on the other side of the cameras.

His tongue slid against hers, and sparks shot through her body. The craving she'd fought so hard to suppress bubbled to the surface, and their mouths met with more primal power than grace. She thought fleetingly of breaking waves, then he pulled her across the mattress with him and she couldn't think at all.

Olivia's hands roved over his body, wanting to touch him everywhere, wanting to dissolve the clothes between them. She tugged him toward her mindlessly, almost surprised when he ended up above her. He pressed against her, not heavy but hard in all the right places, hot and solid and making her feel deliriously feminine.

When he dragged his mouth away from hers, she tried to catch her labored breath, but it only stuck in her lungs as he skimmed his hands under her untucked shirt. His fingers feathered over her rib cage and the band of her bra, up along the swells of her breasts. Her nipples were achingly hard, and she was ablaze in her need to be touched.

But she wanted to touch him, too.

She scrunched his T-shirt upward, revealing the flat planes of his abdomen and the smattering of gold hair across his chest. He pulled back long enough to rip the shirt up over his head. With that accomplished, he glanced meaningfully at her top, and seconds later, it was off, as well. For just a moment, she regretted the unadorned full-coverage bra she wore. How could she compete with the provocative, lacy—

He flicked open the front-closure clasp, pushing the material aside, and what she'd been wearing quickly became a nonissue.

"Beautiful," he said, his normally smooth voice replaced with thick need. He rasped a finger across her nipple, and her already melting body turned a little more liquid.

Framing her breasts with his large hands, he bent his head and sucked one ultrasensitive tip into his mouth, brushing his thumb insistently over the other. The contact spasmed through her body, and her womb clenched.

Without even realizing it, she'd gripped her legs around him. She wedged one hand into the tight back pocket of his jeans, squeezing the firm muscle and grinding him against her. He lifted her breasts closer together, his tongue flicking from one nipple to the other, drawing on them alternately until she was almost writhing beneath him. She was lost in a daze of passion and piercing sensation, her actions guided solely by physical instinct and pleasure.

Her hips lifted off the bed, meeting his, and he raised his face to kiss her, one hand fumbling at the waistband of her slacks. She shimmied free of the confining material and reached for the button on his straining fly. Before tugging the zipper down, she slid her fingertips inside the denim, brushing over his erection, the touch both a tease and a promise.

With obvious reluctance, he moved away from her to pull off his shoes and socks, but there was nothing reluctant about the way he discarded his jeans and briefs in one hurried motion.

Oh, my.

Though she'd already known he was incredibly turned on and plenty well-endowed, seeing him like this, naked, wanting her...she swallowed. He paused to pull his wallet out of his pants, and cool air hit her damp body in his absence. But only Justin could ease her burning.

He seared her with a glance that hinted at naughty nights and hot wet kisses. "Your panties."

The command held just enough playfulness to temper the steel edge of desire in his voice. Once she'd obligingly stripped them off, he returned to kiss her, sucking on her bottom lip, drawing her tongue against his. His fingers passed her hipbone, into the V of her thighs, and parted the slick folds there. Olivia moaned into his mouth.

She'd never been as ready as she was right now, and she bucked against him in wordless encouragement. He sheathed himself in a condom, then positioned himself over her, looking into her eyes for a split second. Meeting his gaze, she knew she'd never want anyone like this again. He entered her in one smooth thrust, and her eyes closed as she gasped.

They moved together, and Olivia's thoughts were nothing more than fragmented sensory perceptions. The sound of their bodies meeting. The taste of salt on her lips. The musky, potent fragrance of sex enveloping them. The mattress creaking softly beneath her, spurring them on. And the feeling—oh, *yes*—of Justin sliding in and out of her, filling her just the right way.

Sensation built, coiling in her clenched muscles and transmitting throughout her body. Closer, closer... Her spine arched as she braced herself for the climax that would send her hurtling into mindless bliss. Then she came, in throbbing relentless tremors. He pushed frantically into her, pumping his hips as he groaned and found his own release.

"Olivia!" He pressed a quick kiss to her lips, then sagged onto the mattress.

Her heart was racing, and she felt as if she could float off into unconsciousness. Time and space had no meaning. It wasn't that she was sleepy, just so sated and relaxed that it would be easy to—

Oh, dear Lord. She couldn't fall asleep here! They shouldn't be here at all. Had they even locked the door? And what did it say about her that she was only just *now* stopping to think about that?

She scooted toward the edge of the bed, but her limp muscles weren't as cooperative as she would have liked. She was still too shaky to stand.

"Olivia?"

"I have to get dressed!" She started to look over her shoulder at him, then decided she couldn't face his nudity—perfect though it was. "*You* have to get dressed. Put something on!"

The mattress shifted, and she knew he'd pushed himself partially upright. "Why the rush? Did you hear someone outside?"

Hear? Oh, no. Had anyone heard them? Heard her?

"It's blind dumb luck that no one interrupted," she said. "We need to get the hell out of here before our luck runs out."

He chuckled softly. "You have an interesting take on 'afterglow.' Relax. Everyone from the shoot's gone, and anyway, we got to do the shoot here because the place is practically deserted right now."

"Practically!" She shot to her feet, struggling into her shirt as she moved. She didn't have the manual dexterity to mess with the bra, and it wouldn't kill her to drive home without one. "I risked my job, the promotion I want, my reputation, my own self-respect on *practically?*"

He stood, too, his tone less amused as he tried to soothe her. "It's all right. No one walked in."

Angry with herself and with his dismissive attitude, she yanked on her underwear and pants. He didn't get it.

Her past was littered with heartaches that could mostly be traced to foolish romantic impulses on her part. So she'd resolved to be wiser and more disciplined. And what had happened? She'd wrapped up a shoot with a hot quickie with the photographer!

This was a man she worked with, a man who'd told her in South Carolina he was entitled to selfish me-time, a man who seemed interested in a different woman every time she saw him.

Even though Justin had experience with how quickly a female's mood could change, he was stunned. He knew beyond a shadow of a doubt that Olivia had been as sexually satisfied as humanly possible, yet now she was cramming her bra into her purse with angry, jerky movements.

Once he had his jeans on, he circled the bed and walked to her. He wanted to put his arms around her, but it seemed best not to yet. "Talk to me, sweetheart."

"Please don't call me that." Her eyes flashed at him. "I...we're not sweethearts."

"We're lovers." What had happened between them had been staggering.

Sex had never been like that before. Nothing had ever been like that before. He'd known Olivia burned hotter than most people would guess by looking at her, but he still hadn't been prepared for the intensity of making love to her.

"No!" Almost as if dreading he might try to hold her, she shuffled backward. "I mean, yes, we were, but this isn't going to happen again."

"What?" He couldn't imagine anything that would have shocked him more than that one vehement statement.

Was this the same woman who'd asked in her office whether he'd wanted companionship or sex? And now *she* was drawing the line at a one-night stand? She hadn't even given them a full night.

"Olivia, I know this was...unplanned, but—"

"Insane." She threw her hands in the air, her voice

slightly hysterical. "This was insane. Maybe this sort of thing happens so often to you that you can be nonchalant about spontaneous sex with a co-worker."

Could she have been further off base about his life?

"But I don't do stuff like this," she continued. "I promised myself I wouldn't. Do you know what you are?"

"Confused."

"Chocolate. You are walking chocolate."

Most women he knew enjoyed chocolate, yet the way she said it made him sound more like a walking disease.

"I fell off the wagon, but it was a one-time mistake," she said. "I need salad, and you're...an éclair!"

Interesting choice of phallic metaphors. "Look, Olivia, why don't we get out of here and go talk about this?"

"I just want to go home."

At one time, this might have been his idea of heaven—great sex with Olivia, then going their separate ways into the sunset. The joke was on him, though, because the thought of her leaving and their never touching one another again....

"You won't even hear me out?"

"There's nothing to say. This isn't me, Justin."

He raised an eyebrow. "It's more 'you' than you think it is. No, don't get angry. I'm not suggesting you usually fall into bed on a whim, I'm certain you don't. But you can't hide from your own passionate nature."

"A person's nature can be changed," she told him, squaring her shoulders. "I was able to eradicate one set of bad habits over a decade in the making. I can do it again."

He resented being called a bad habit. "I—"

"Don't. The truth is, I have a date, not tonight, but this weekend, with a man who's a sensible choice for me. I think we'll be compatible."

The image of her with another man, so soon after what he himself had just shared with her, caused him to see red. "A sensible choice? Is that code for one more thing you can hide behind?"

She flinched. "Goodbye, Justin."

Her words were symbolic of course. It wasn't as though he'd never see her again. Yet the farewell seemed eerily final as she ducked out the door.

OLIVIA WAS SITTING at her desk feeling faintly nauseous when Jeanie knocked on the door Wednesday morning.

"Hey," the receptionist began in breezy greeting. Her tone quickly changed as she took in Olivia's appearance. "Yikes. You don't look so good."

"However bad I look, I feel worse." She hadn't been able to sleep last night. She'd been torn between wanting to cry, wanting to eat everything in the house and wanting to call Justin.

Jeanie sat down. "Should you go home for the day? There's a bug going around, you know. Are you running a fever?"

No, she and Justin had broken the fever that had consumed her—funny, she didn't feel any better. She'd considered calling in sick, but what was the point? Unless Sweet Nothings suddenly opened a branch in

Walla Walla and transferred one of them, she'd have to face Justin sometime. Besides, after all that nonsense he'd spouted yesterday about her hiding...

"I'm fine, Jeanie. I just had a rough night." Actually, what she'd had was the most sexually exquisite evening of her life.

"Well, I hate to tell you this since it feels like kicking you while you're down, but I have some bad news."

"This is as good a time as any to hit me with it." It wasn't as though she would feel any worse.

"Mark can't make it."

Should she know who Mark was? "Can't make what?"

"Dinner, Saturday." Jeanie peered at her with concern. "Mark, the doctor? Albert's brother. There was a last-minute shift in the schedule, so it turns out he'll be on call all weekend."

She was being punished.

The truth was, even though she'd dutifully asked Jeanie to follow through with the blind-date arrangements, Olivia had lacked sincere enthusiasm. But she'd told herself she hadn't originally been enthusiastic about jogging or abdominal crunches, either, and she was always happier after going through with them. Now, with her resolve to make sensible choices redoubled, she was losing her first real opportunity.

"What about before the weekend?" she asked desperately. "What about tomorrow? Tonight, even!"

Jeanie's eyebrows shot up. "Well...I could ask. To be honest, I wasn't sure your heart was really in it."

"It is. I swear." She still couldn't believe what had happened yesterday, but it had been the eye-opener she needed. Her whole life, she'd been drawn to things notoriously bad for her, and she had too many emotional bruises to subscribe to the "if-it-feels-good-do-him" motto.

By midmorning, Jeanie reported back with the happy news that Mark appreciated Olivia's understanding about his schedule and would love to have dinner with her that evening, if she was available.

"Great." Relief swept through her. "I—I'm really looking forward to it."

Dating sensible guys was like giving up chocolate. The initial cravings stage was difficult, but after kicking the bad habit, a person often found she'd genuinely lost her taste for it.

In theory.

MEG PUSHED open the steel exit door, her voice echoing in the strange acoustics of the parking garage. "I still can't believe this elevator boycott of yours."

"Taking the stairs is good for us," Olivia said lamely, pretty sure she wasn't fooling anyone.

The two of them were en route to lunch, and Meg was lamenting the fact she still didn't have a date for Friday's fashion show. "It wouldn't be so bad, but I don't have a killer dress, either. You have to have one or the other, a hot guy or a great outfit. Preferably both."

Olivia laughed, but it was a hollow sound.

"Hey, maybe if you and Mark hit it off tonight—"

"I'm not asking him to the fashion show," Olivia interrupted. "It's a formal event, and it's two days away.

Besides, Jeanie said something about him being on call this weekend."

"You have any other prospects?" Meg asked as they crossed the first few rows of cars, toward her sporty red convertible.

A pang struck Olivia midsection as she wondered if Justin would have a date...and what it would have been like to be that date. "Well, Chad did seem awfully interested yesterday, but I can't imagine what would induce me to go anywhere with him."

"Chad Langley?" Meg grimaced. "Yecch."

"I couldn't have said it better." As far as potential men for her dating diet, Chad was nothing but empty calories. Empty everything, really.

A car zipped past them, and just as they reached Meg's parking spot, the other driver pulled into the free space next to her. When Justin climbed out of the sedan, Olivia's knees shook. She wasn't ready to see him yet!

But he barely looked at her. "Ladies," he said directly to Meg. Then without another word, he headed toward the building.

Meg's head whipped around so quickly, Olivia expected to hear something snap. "You want to tell me what *that* was about?"

Olivia opened the passenger door. "What do you mean?"

"That man couldn't have given you a colder shoulder if he were a penguin. You said the shoot yesterday went well."

"It did. I really think Steve will like the pictures." She hoped, anyway.

Meg started the car. "Did you and Justin argue?"

More like the opposite. "Things might be a little awkward because we, um, kissed."

"And you didn't mention this sooner? I ought to make you walk."

"It was no big deal. He was sort of helping me discourage Chad, and he wanted Tony to know he wasn't gay." Technically, she was telling the truth, even if the kiss hadn't taken place until *after* everyone else had left.

"So you've worked with Justin twice now, and you've ended up kissing him...help me with the math here...oh yes, twice. Any plans to continue this pattern?"

"Absolutely not!" Then again, Olivia hadn't planned on the first two times, either. "Besides, yesterday was more like a—a mutual favor."

"Good sex always has been, girlfriend."

A squeak escaped Olivia. "Sex? Who said anything about sex? I never said we had— God, Meg, I had sex with Justin Hawthorne. What was I thinking?"

"Oh, honey." Meg's eyes widened, but good friend that she was, she took the confession in stride. "There's an ice-cream place on the corner. You want to skip lunch and just go there?"

"No." Olivia sighed, proud of herself for resisting temptation, even if the willpower came too little, too late. "Cellulite is not the answer."

"Wanna blow off this afternoon and go spend lots of money on faboo outfits for Friday?"

"*Now* you're talking."

11

OLIVIA FINISHED buttoning her blouse and glanced at the digital clock on her nightstand—ten minutes until her date was due to pick her up. She actually wished he'd show up early. Spare time to think wasn't what she needed today.

Her lifestyle was conservative enough that she'd never had a date with a man the day after having fantastic sex with another, and she was nervous. She had to get back on track, and dinner with Mark was a step in the right direction.

With a few minutes to kill, she decided she should cut the tags off the new dress hanging on the back of her door and put it in the closet. Meg had wanted her to buy an audacious burgundy number with a sheer top, but Olivia had chosen a can't-go-wrong black cocktail dress. As she crossed the room, she caught her reflection in her peripheral vision and stopped suddenly, glancing at the mirror above her dresser.

Since she wasn't focusing on something specific, like whether or not her hair was frizzy or applying blush evenly, it was the general impression she noticed. She had what would politely be called a "classic" look. Her hair, worn long in the same basic style she'd had since high school, fell past the shoulders of a conventional outfit that was neat if not memorable.

Boring, Olivia. The description you're dancing around is boring.

Whether or not Mark turned out to be the social equivalent of a bland-but-healthy lima bean, *she* certainly was, wasn't she? She'd spent so much of yesterday watching the seductive models strut their stuff in lacy lingerie, wishing she were more like them, that now she couldn't help but wonder why she *wasn't*. The words Justin had snapped at her as she'd left bubbled up from her subconscious to the surface of her mind— he'd accused her of hiding. She'd tried to ignored his remark, but, alone with only her reflection, she found she couldn't.

Obviously, she wasn't going to dinner in a silk teddy, but why had she worked so hard for so long to get her body into its current shape only to conceal it in high-necked tops, long skirts and practically genderless pantsuits? *Conceal* being another word for hide.

Dazed, Olivia made eye contact with the woman in the mirror, feeling as though she was seeing her for the first time. She had to own something more feminine, more striking. Come to think of it, what was stopping her from wearing a silk teddy? No one would know what was under her clothes. No one else *needed* to know; this was for her.

Sinking down onto her bed, she thought about the past few weeks. She'd been changing, from the small rebellions of ordering pizza and altering layouts at the last minute to yesterday's dizzying sexual encounter. Was it Justin? Was this his bad influence? He'd definitely seen something in her that others hadn't, but she'd been ready to change. Even her now-faded anger with Sean had been a sign of evolution. There'd been a time when, instead of being rightfully angry, she would have wondered deep down if his unfaithfulness signaled something lacking in her.

I'm not lacking. If nothing else, yesterday had helped her see that. She and Justin had shared a raw, forceful passion that had overtaken him as much as her. Maybe she needed to be more careful about when and how she let impulses affect her, but burying herself in boring wasn't truly what she wanted. Why hadn't she seen that before?

She stripped in a rush, and by the time her doorbell rang, Olivia was satisfied with her appearance. She'd donned the skirt she'd worn to Hewitt's Bar, the one that showed off legs shaped by devoted exercise, and she seemed to have discovered a good makeup regimen for her. Minimal without being bland. She'd used very few cosmetics, but what she had applied went mostly to making her eyes more vivid and dramatic.

She could be dramatic. Who knew?

Swinging open the front door, she thought to herself that if Mark liked "exotic women," to quote Jeanie, it was fortunate she'd opted out of the sensible pantsuit accessorized with lip gloss and a ponytail. At first glance, though, Mark hardly seemed the "exotic" type. As cute as he'd been in his picture, the real-life version of Mark stood almost an inch shorter than Olivia, looking slightly out of place in a blue pinstriped shirt and a pale-yellow tie.

It's a nice suit. And a man doesn't have to be taller than you to be sexy.

While that was true, she couldn't help thinking that

if the occasion ever arose, she wouldn't fit as well with Mark as she—

"You must be Mark. Nice to finally meet you after everything Jeanie's told me."

The man smiled shyly. "I hope she didn't build me up too much. She certainly didn't exaggerate about you. You look great."

"Thank you. So do you."

"I spend so much time in scrubs, I hardly know what to wear out in public anymore." He fidgeted with his tie, probably to straighten it, although he ended up knocking it more askew.

She stepped out onto the front porch with him, jacket and purse in hand, pausing only long enough to lock her door.

"I know this is rude for a first date," he said apologetically, "but I have to leave my beeper on tonight. One of my favorite patients is due, and with this being her first, she's pretty nervous. Not to worry, though, I don't anticipate dinner being interrupted. Poor woman's been contracting all week, but her cervix isn't even ripe yet. I checked just a few hours ago."

Olivia's footing faltered on the brick walkway outside her apartment. Call her a pessimist, but she didn't have a great feeling about any date that began with conversation about another woman's cervix.

Most women were happy to find a good OB/ GYN...but across the dinner table on the first date she'd had in over a month?

Stop it. Give him a fair chance. His profession was a wonderfully respected one, and it wasn't going to keep her from being attracted to him.

What *was* likely to keep her from being attracted was the fact that he wasn't Justin Hawthorne.

"SO DINNER wasn't exactly the time of your life?" From the other side of the desk, Meg clucked her tongue sympathetically.

"Technically, we didn't make it as far as dinner. Tammy went into labor halfway through the appetizers, and the good doctor had to run." Olivia sighed as she thought about the prematurely halted date the night before—his exit had been a relief. "To be honest, I think Jeanie made a misdiagnosis. Other than the fact we can both be painfully shy, we didn't seem to have much in common." And Olivia had been preoccupied with another man, which never boded well for the direction of an evening.

"Well, take heart," Meg advised. "You—"

Bzzt. The interoffice line on her phone beeped, and Olivia pressed a finger to the flashing red button. "Olivia Lockhart."

Steve's voice reverberated through the speaker phone. "Liv, why don't you pop into my office before lunch today? We need to talk."

Olivia swallowed nervously, panic leaving a bitter taste in her mouth. She had the guilty fleeting notion that maybe he'd somehow found out she'd used a professionally leased setting for a wild tryst. "S-sure."

Once Steve was off the line, Meg shook her head. "I know what you're thinking, but he probably just wants to talk to you about the fashion show. How mad could he really be about one or two shots?"

"What?"

"Isn't that what you were thinking?" Meg bit her lip. "I thought you were worried because you more or less took Stormy and Chad out of some of those photos."

"No, that wasn't what I was concerned about, but thanks. It is now."

"You know, I should really go back to my own office. I spend entirely too much time in here."

A few hours later, Olivia was thrilled to discover she *didn't* have anything to worry about. She floated out of Steve's office on a cloud, perhaps making history by leaving a meeting with her boss in a fabulous mood.

I'm getting the promotion!

He hadn't said it point-blank, but there was no longer any doubt. When Steve had called her in, he'd asked her about the very set of B and B pictures Meg had mentioned, where the lingerie had been featured without actually being seen on the model. Olivia's heart sank as she anticipated a reprimand for wasting time or film on something that contradicted their product-on-the-people policy.

Instead, Steve had congratulated her for coming up with such an effective idea on the spur of the moment and going with what worked, despite what had been agreed upon in the office. "That's the take-charge attitude we're looking for in a Design Supervisor, Liv."

By the end of the meeting, it was so obvious the promotion was hers that she expected to have lunch with him so they could settle the specifics. But he'd left it at confirming she'd be at the fashion show tomorrow night and coyly hinting that the event might be even more special for her than for everyone else at Sweet Nothings. She couldn't believe she—

Thud.

Ow. Olivia had been so caught up in her good news and looking forward to the fashion show she hadn't realized someone was walking out of the HR suite. The collision had squashed her nose against the front of a man's dark blue pullover, and the scent of familiar cologne told her who she'd bumped into well before she glanced up to see Justin's strained expression.

She teetered backward. "Sorry."

"No problem." He reached out to help steady her, and the contact of his fingers on her shoulder zinged through her with electric force. Having ensured she wasn't going to topple over, he sidestepped her.

"Justin, wait!"

He paused, his expression wary.

"Can I...would you like to have lunch with me?"

There was so much she wanted to tell him, not just about the promotion, but about his being a little bit right about her. She wasn't sure what a relationship with him would be like, wasn't sure if that was even what he wanted, but she realized she'd been wrong to ignore the opportunity to find out.

His eyebrows shot up at the invitation. "You want to have—wait, you look different today."

"Just something I did with my eye makeup. No biggie." But she was pleased he'd noticed. Meg and Jeanie hadn't.

"You look great. Am I allowed to say that, or is that too *chocolate* of me?"

Olivia could feel herself blushing at his sardonic tone. "I hurt your feelings."

"It may come as a surprise to you, but I do have them."

"I reacted badly," she admitted. "The whole thing just caught me off guard."

The corner of his mouth lifted in the beginning of a grin. "Well, you weren't the only one. I guess the big difference between us is that I *like* those kinds of surprises. The lunch invitation was a nice surprise, too."

"Then you'll join me? I wanted to tell you—"

Inside the HR suite, someone fired up the copier, and the noise of the machine printing off documents reminded Olivia of how public their location was. Somehow, Justin always managed to make her feel as though they were isolated in their own private little bubble.

"Tell me what?" he prompted.

"Let's get out of here, first." She trusted Justin's discretion, but she shouldn't be talking about the unannounced promotion here. "Come with me?"

He grinned wickedly. "That's the best offer I've had all day."

When they got to the elevator doors, Justin sent her a sidelong glance. "Rather take the stairs?"

Had he noticed her office avoidance of the elevators? "Nope. This'll be just fine."

"You're sure?"

Desire and apprehension collided, and she squared her shoulders. "I'm getting there."

JUSTIN IMMEDIATELY reached for the check the waitress set on the sun-bathed table.

"Don't even think about it," he told Olivia. "We're celebrating your promotion. Unofficially, of course."

"Thank you." She smiled at him, looking inordinately bashful for a woman who'd flirted all through lunch.

"You're welcome." He was thankful, too, for her apparent change of heart.

When she'd walked out of that B and B suite two days ago, he'd begun reevaluating his outlook. Next Thursday, he'd be thirty years old. Since Andrea had left for college, Justin had based what he thought he wanted on the plans for his freedom he'd devised at twenty-two. For nearly a decade, he'd told himself he'd regain lost time, but he'd been finding that his needs and wants now just weren't the same as they'd been eight years ago.

Ye gods, had he *matured?*

Nah, he still wanted hot sex and lots of spontaneity and fun—he just wanted it with the woman seated across from him now. And after the lunch they'd just shared, he nursed hopes Olivia might actually want the same.

"That was fabulous." Leaning her head back, she closed her eyes and basked in the sunlight streaming through the floor-to-ceiling window. "I hate to go back to the office, but I've already had one inexcusably long lunch this week."

"And it wouldn't do for the new Design Supervisor to start blowing off her work," he teased as he handed the waitress the signed credit card receipt.

"Design Supervisor." Olivia grinned at the title. "I can't wait to call my folks tonight and tell them."

They'd talked some about her parents, and it was obvious she came from a close-knit family. When conversation had turned to his own relatives, he'd explained his parents had been killed in a boating accident, but he hadn't gone much beyond that. She knew about his younger sisters without all the details of Justin's saga of raising two teenage girls. Today was about Olivia.

As they walked toward the entrance of the restaurant, Olivia craned her head back to look up at him. "We talked all about my job, tell me about being a photographer."

"Well, photo shoots have unexpected perks," he drawled, confident she no longer viewed Tuesday as the biggest mistake of her life. Did this mean he was no longer—how had she put it?—an éclair?

She shot him a look of mock reprimand. "I meant, how did you get into photography, what drew you to it?"

"Domination." He grinned. "I like taking a moment and capturing it, making it somehow uniquely mine, even if its only through the use of a certain aperture. I like the challenge of getting others to see something the way I see it."

He held the door open for her. "I'd love to take your picture sometime."

"My picture?" Even though he believed Olivia would have resisted the unflinching scrutiny of being photographed a week ago, she now chuckled at the suggestion. "Would that be in the studio-portrait sense, or the drop-the-robe-Ms.-Lockhart, kind of way?"

He was delighted with her playful tone. This was the

side of her he'd wanted to see her let out more—the side he'd told her she couldn't keep repressing. Was her buoyant mood and confidence due to winning her promotion, or was there more to her uncharacteristically mischievous grin? "I'm not picky, so the robe is completely up to you."

"I guess that'll depend," she teased.

He wasn't sure what exactly it depended on, but he couldn't wait to find out.

"Hey."

Olivia glanced up from the file cabinet, where she'd been muttering the alphabet song under her breath because she'd temporarily blanked on whether or not *O* came before *Q*. With the fashion show tonight, the dress she'd exchanged last night and her determination to see where things with Justin led, she was preoccupied and jittery. She wanted to follow her heart, but hopeful optimism was at war with past experience.

Justin's tender smile went a long way toward reassuring her, though. Her heart did a slow somersault at the sight of him.

"Hi." She shut the drawer and leaned against the cabinet for support.

Shifting his weight, he rested one hand at the pocket of his charcoal trousers. "It's not a big deal, but I had something I wanted to give you."

"Really?"

He picked up a small bag, brown paper with twine handles, from the floor just outside her doorway. "Just a little good luck for tonight."

He walked toward her and stopped when he was close enough to slip the bag's handles over her fingers.

She made a fist, capturing his hand as well as the unexpected gift. "You didn't have to do this."

"I know."

Even though they'd had a great time at lunch yesterday, he hadn't kissed her since Tuesday, and his nearness now was driving her crazy. She didn't want to let go of him—wanted to pull him much closer, as a matter of fact—but she was incredibly curious to find out what was in the bag. Based on gifts from men in her past and the fact that Justin got the same employee discount as anyone else at Sweet Nothings, she half expected lingerie.

If so, did he know she'd be happy to model it for him after the show tonight?

She pushed aside the single sheet of white tissue paper that was shoved guy-style into the bag and discovered a plain silver frame resting at the bottom. It held an oversized postcard of a Kallie Carmichael painting, one of the Rebirth series. Just right for her desk here or her bookshelf at home. The man was sexy as hell, but he could be genuinely kind, too. And after some of the men in her past, that made him all the sexier.

"Thank you. This—" When she glanced up, he was too close for her to remember how to breathe.

Her stomach fluttered. The vibrant shades of green in the mini-Carmichael print had nothing on Justin's eyes. Why had she ever thought she had a chance of resisting this man? She certainly didn't want to resist anymore. Before she'd even realized she'd moved, she was pushing up on her tiptoes, raising her face toward his.

Justin's eyes widened, but any surprise he felt didn't stop him from acting. His hands came to her shoulders, and he hauled her to him as his mouth met hers. It was the first time she'd initiated a kiss between the two of them, and she experienced a heady rush of sensual power. He didn't push, letting her set the pace, and, teasing her as much as him, she kept it slow and gentle at first. Just their lips, caressing, nibbling, sucking lightly. Then she stabbed her tongue into his mouth, greedily making up for the time that had passed since they'd last touched one another.

His hands had dropped below her waist, cupping her backside, and he dragged her against the rigid length of his sex. She moved against him once, then again, heatedly, before realizing they hadn't even shut the office door.

Shuddering with the effort it took to do so, she pulled out of his arms. They were to the side of her office door, hidden from the view of casual passersby, but if anyone had poked their head in the doorway, they would have received quite an eyeful.

"I don't know what is wrong with me," she said.

"Not a thing," he assured her. "That was damn near perfect."

"No, I—" She shot him a pointed glance. "Maybe we should have this conversation on opposite sides of the desk. I need to keep my hands off you."

He scowled. "This isn't where you call me an éclair again, is it? Because—"

"No, it's just that Tuesday we didn't think to lock the

door, and now I didn't even close the door. We work here, for God's sake! You make me forget..." Everything, except how much she wanted him. "You should go."

"I suppose you're right," he said, running a hand through his hair. "If I stay, I'll just want to kiss you more. But I'll see you tonight?"

Wordless with anticipation, she nodded.

He paused at the door and glanced over his shoulder. "Start thinking now about whether or not you want a kiss good-night. And whether you're going to want one good morning."

12

IN ANOTHER quarter of an hour, the show would begin and one beautiful woman after another would sashay down the catwalk in barely there confections, but in Justin's opinion, none of them could hold a candle to the stunning lady who'd just walked through the door of the spacious hotel ballroom.

The wine-colored dress Olivia wore was a playful nod to the lingerie they were promoting. The cap sleeves and scooped neckline were made of a sheer mesh in a lighter hue of the solid velvet outlining her breasts. The material over her midriff and navel was see-through before angling into a formfitting velvet skirt that stopped right below her knees. There was probably a specific name for that length, but who cared about fashion terminology when Olivia was walking around as if she'd stepped out of a fantasy?

Her eyes were wide and smoky, and her hair was pulled back into some kind of complicated knot that left her face and neck completely exposed. She was so feminine and sexy his body tensed with need.

After their first kiss, she'd been skittish and obviously regretful; after they'd made love, she'd fled. He desired her, intensely, but the next move had to come from her. He'd told her to think about what she wanted to happen between them tonight, now all he could do was hope the decision she'd made was the one he longed for so badly.

Then her silvery eyes, brighter and more dazzling than ever, found his through the crowd, and he knew for certain how much she wanted him, too. Her expression, her very body language, telegraphed the same passion burning inside him. He murmured an apology as he jostled some partygoers on his way to meet his lover.

Olivia smiled when he reached her, her gaze pure mischief. "Hi."

Was it too soon for them to leave? "You look amazing. That dress...."

"Thank you. You're pretty easy on the eyes, too." She tilted her head back, her eyes locked with his. Then, she slowly glanced downward, appreciatively taking in everything from the shoulders of his black jacket to the polished tips of his shoes, pausing meaningfully in the areas between that piqued her interest.

Justin was rock-hard by the time she looked back to his face.

She was still the woman he'd worked with, laughed with and admired, the woman he'd kissed until she melted in his arms, but tonight she also seemed more, a woman exuding raw, feminine power. Nothing nervous or skittish about her.

A circulating waiter passed with a tray of delicious finger foods, and Olivia selected a small puff pastry. She held it to her lips, darting just the tip of her tongue out to taste the dollop of filling, then sucking gently before pushing the morsel into her mouth with her finger.

Her eyes were heavy-lidded with sensory pleasure, and Justin throbbed with need.

She strolled toward the table where drinks were being served, and he followed along for the ride.

"I've decided to be more proactive," she said.

Proactive was good.

"You know the ex-boyfriend I told you about?"

The imbecile who'd looked at another woman when he could have had Olivia? "I remember."

"I've always been like a bystander in my own love life. I sort of tumbled in and out of relationships. Even the date I had this week—"

Justin's gut clenched with possessiveness as he pictured her with another man.

"—it was something Meg and Jeanie talked me into. I'm getting this promotion because I displayed take-charge capabilities. So it occurred to me, why am I so passive in my personal life? Life is something to be experienced, right?"

"Absolutely." He handed her a champagne flute and grabbed an imported beer for himself. "I'm here to help in any way I can."

"You're so thoughtful." She grinned, but for a second her teasing expression flickered, softened. "Actually, you've helped me a lot already. Thank you."

If she was crediting him for her evolving attitude, he thought she was underestimating herself. But he returned her grin. "I don't suppose this gratitude comes with tangible rewards?"

She shot him a sly smile and sipped her champagne. Then she looked up. "You've probably never dieted, have you? More women do than men. Do you know some experts say it's actually beneficial to indulge yourself sometimes? But I don't. Before, I never treated myself to milk shakes and stolen kisses. I never let myself enjoy the decadent things in life."

He was so mesmerized by the way her finger slowly traced the rim of the crystal flute in her hands he had trouble focusing on her words.

"Do you know what I *really* want, Justin? What I'd like to savor?"

If she named a dessert food, he was going to cry. "Tell me."

"You. Tonight."

He hadn't even realized he was holding his breath until he let it out in a relieved whoosh. Her words rolled through his body, lava-hot, obliterating everything else.

Suddenly the music playing in the ballroom stopped, and Steve Reynolds tapped on a microphone at the front of the catwalk. "Ladies and gentlemen, welcome to the third annual Sweet Nothings fashion show!"

Applause thundered through the room.

"If you'll find your seats, we'll get started."

Justin leaned down, letting his mouth brush across Olivia's ear, loving the way she shivered at the contact. "Any chance we can sneak out now?"

Her laugh was rueful. "The company announcements won't be made until after the show, and it'll be pretty obvious if I'm not here for them."

He was supposed to keep his hands off of her for hours? Worse, he was expected to photograph parts of the show, and he was certain he wouldn't be able to concentrate on the models. "It's going to be a long night."

Olivia turned to wink at him. "That's the plan—a *very* long night."

TONIGHT WAS a dream, Olivia thought as she applied a coat of lipstick she hoped didn't stay on long. She glanced into the mirror of the ladies' lounge, marveling at the surrealness of the evening—her uncharacteristic boldness, the sexy man hanging on her every word and glance, her professional success topping off a night that was already perfection. She planned to enjoy the magic as long as it lasted, stretching out each sublime moment.

She was proud of her reflection. The confidence in her appearance that had started mostly as a bluff had somehow become reality, even if it was only temporary. As someone who'd "blossomed" early in life and had spent years trying to subdue her curves, she normally eschewed anything that drew attention to her chest, but she loved the dress she was wearing. More, she loved the way Justin watched her. His unmistakable passion made it that much easier to be candid about what she wanted.

Moments ago, she'd received her promotion in front of a packed house, charged with adrenaline after a great show, and in her brief speech, she'd been wittier than she'd ever been outside a few sarcastic conversations with Meg. Who was this new Olivia and why hadn't she made an appearance before now?

"I can't believe you're in here!"

Olivia turned to grin at her friend. "Speak of the devil. I was just thinking about you."

"Then you should get your head examined." Meg glanced underneath the doors of empty stalls, then balled up her fists at the waist of her sequined dress in a posture of good-natured chastisement. "The hottest man in the building is out there waiting for you. I'd be thinking about *him*."

"I was doing some of that, too."

"The looks you two have been exchanging violate fire codes. I guess you won't be staying at the party long?"

"Well, I didn't want to rush *right* out after the big announcement." Plus, now that she knew for sure what was going to happen tonight, she had to admit there was a certain excitement in the anticipation. This was so different from the spontaneous encounter on Tuesday. The passionate impulsiveness had been incredible, but knowing ahead of time, looking forward to his touch, to their making love, was enticing, too.

Meg smirked. "Bet you're glad now you came to your senses and got the dress I suggested."

As she envisioned Justin removing that dress, Olivia's heart beat a little faster. "On second thought, we probably *will* be going soon."

Olivia left the lounge and found Justin standing at a tall, skinny round table without chairs. He'd stowed his camera equipment in his car and got them fresh drinks. She squeezed in a little closer to him, nervous, but in a good way.

"The show was a smashing success," she said over the pulsating music her co-workers were dancing to on the makeshift floor. "Did you get some good pictures?"

"Probably not. I may have had the lens cap on all night."

She made a tut-tut sound. "And here I thought you were this brilliant photographer."

"I had other things on my mind." His hungry gaze made her body tingle. Why had she fought the attraction she felt for so long?

"For instance?" she teased.

"I'll show you." His hand tightened around hers. "Walk with me? The courtyard's supposed to be beautiful."

Knowing they wouldn't be going back inside made her knees go weak. They stopped at the coat check so she could get her jacket, but Justin would provide the real warmth she needed.

Fortunately, other partygoers were dissuaded by the cold and stayed inside with the music and refreshments. An ornate pattern of wrought iron fenced in the courtyard on all sides except for the gothic entrance, made up of columns and a stone archway. The area was lovely, with its brick pathways, majestic trees strung with tiny white lights, and the gurgling fountain in the center. What Olivia most appreciated about her surroundings was that they were almost deserted.

On the far side, one couple sat on a stone bench, but from this distance, Olivia couldn't tell if they were people she knew. Still, she wound her way toward one of the impressive columns, stopping in its shadow when she felt hidden from the view of casual passersby.

Justin dropped one hand to her waist, the other

brushing across her bangs. "Did I tell you already how terrific you look?"

She leaned forward until her body met his. He was turned slightly so that she bumped against his hip, but she wanted to feel him pressed against her. Wanted to revel in this freedom she'd never felt before.

"You did." And now was not the time for more talking.

Olivia angled her head back and pushed up on the balls of her feet, the euphoria she was experiencing heightened by everything from the promotion she'd received to the warm glow of champagne in her system—but mostly the nearness of the man she hadn't stopped wanting since she'd first seen him. He more than met her halfway. His mouth slanted across hers, and the uncharacteristic new wildness she'd been feeling exploded inside her. She thrust her tongue against his, greedy for him and feverish to have him explore her.

Still kissing her, Justin pulled her closer to him, and she couldn't help the feline way she rubbed against him. His hand slid between their bodies, across the sensitive skin of her throat, over her collarbone, to dip inside the sheer neckline of her dress. He brushed his fingertips across her cleavage, caressing the swells of breasts lifted in offering by the top's built-in bra. Her nipples tightened, and her body pulsed with excitement.

She was breathless when they ended the kiss, and his mouth chased the path his fingers had taken, stopping to lave the hollow at the base of her throat, tasting the valley between her breasts. What she was wearing didn't have much give to it, though, and both of them were frustrated with the lack of access.

Then again, this might not be the place to tear off each other's clothes.

"I live half an hour from here," she said. "You?"

His voice was ragged. "Forty-five minutes."

"Too far."

"We'll get a room."

She nodded, already following him to the hotel's entrance. Time had warped itself somehow, both slowing and speeding up simultaneously. Justin's signing them in and leading her to their floor passed in a dazed blur of expectation, yet each second of not having him touch her stood out as a separate agonizing moment.

Olivia could have wept with relief when he opened the door to an eighth-floor bedroom suite with a king-size bed, whirlpool tub and private balcony. The lush environment was nothing more than an aphrodisiac with central heating. She kicked off her shoes, then stood at the partial wall separating the main room from the entryway and bathroom, surveying the surroundings.

"I don't even know where to start." Just looking at the ice bucket gave her ideas.

He moved toward her with lithe, predatory grace. "I do."

His hands fell to her shoulders, and Olivia raised her face, expecting to be kissed again. Instead he turned her around, taking a moment to find the zipper encased in a fold of fabric.

He caught her earlobe between his teeth, his words tickling her. "I want to see you."

The metallic scrape of the zipper echoed off the walls—or maybe just in her head—and a slight draft hit her exposed back. She'd been naked in front of him before, of course, but there'd been nothing premeditated about that. Now, her muscles bunched at the thought of Justin, fully dressed, studying her at his leisure. She'd always been more prone to high necklines and low hems than exhibitionism, but tonight she wanted to be seen, wanted to be uninhibited.

Taking his time, he edged her sleeves down her arms, pausing to rub his thumbs against her, massaging her shoulders. She did a little shimmy, giving the dress the help it needed to slide over her curves in a velvet caress before pooling at her feet, leaving her in only panties and stockings.

Justin sucked in his breath, and she managed to hold herself immobile, trying to picture herself through his eyes—her creamy skin a pale contrast to the dark hair she wore off her neck, the curve of her butt beneath tiny black lacy panties that held gartered stockings in place. She turned slowly, behaving as she had in the ballroom earlier, faking confidence until it slowly became real. The expression of fierce longing on his face made it clear he was more than happy with what he saw.

She teased him with her smile as she ran a hand over the top of the silk stockings. "They're from our signature collection. You like?"

He flashed a promising grin. "I've never been so proud to be a Sweet Nothings employee."

As her original nervousness subsided, she felt completely decadent in her undressed state. During the

B and B shoot, she'd imagined wearing lingerie for him, capturing his attention and reveling in his passion, and now she was living the fantasy. But she wanted to see him, too, to feel his skin against hers and lose herself in the sensations they could only create together.

She eased his jacket off his shoulders, but when she reached for the buttons on his shirt, he surprised her by lightly catching her wrists. Tantalized by the possibilities of where he might touch her, she obligingly raised her arms above her head, letting him hold them loosely against the wall with one hand. The combination of arousal and cool air had her nipples puckered and erect, but his free hand moved past her breasts without stopping.

He trailed downward, traveling over her belly button, swirling featherlight circles over her abdomen that made her shiver inside. Then, staring deeply into her eyes, he moved past the satin triangle of her panties and drew one finger across the material between her legs, sliding back and forth until the fabric was slippery with her moisture.

Her body trembled at the repeated movement, and a soft breathy cry escaped her. He let go of her wrists and brought his hands to her breasts. Wedging his leg between her own, he rolled one nipple between his fingers and drew the other deep into his mouth. Her blood pounded in her ears, and need ricocheted through her. She tunneled her hands through his hair, holding him close.

He slipped his hand beneath the elastic band of her panties, caressing her in ways that left her gripping him for support before he easily pressed one finger inside her, then another. She arched against the wall, adrift in the moment and Justin's sensual mastery, suspended in time until her body coiled and exploded in quaking spasms that made her crave more even as they eased her initial need.

She clutched his shoulders through the first waves wracking her body, then began fumbling with his clothes once her orgasm had subsided to manageable tremors. Justin moved to help her, and in a series of frenzied actions, they made it to the bed, shedding garments as they went. When at last they were both naked, she paused, taking more time to study him than she had the first time they'd made love.

He was incredible. A marble likeness of him in the courtyard they'd visited earlier would be considered high art. Male perfection, from the strong set of his jaw to the proud erection that made her body quiver all over again.

Their kisses were carnal, and the abandon Olivia experienced was unprecedented. Her desire for him was too strong to allow any inhibitions to stop her from taking what she wanted. Running her fingers over him, alternately stroking and raking her nails lightly across him, she dropped kisses across his chest, working her way lower.

Justin was delighted to give her free rein, but watching her climax at his touch had been erotic enough to push him to his limits. Having her lips close around him, pulling him into the damp, silky suction of her mouth, nearly sent him to his own release.

He groaned. What she was doing was beyond unbelievable, but he was dying to make love to her, wanted them to come together. "Olivia, if you don't stop now, we—"

"Condoms?"

"Pants pocket."

She slid off the bed while he lay on his back, counting to ten and trying to bring his body back from the brink of rapture. Pushing himself up on his elbow, he reached for the first foil packet.

Olivia shook her head. "I'm exercising my take-charge option."

I've died and gone to heaven. "Any plans to be gentle with me?"

She grinned. "None whatsoever."

His heart stopped when she unrolled the condom over his throbbing erection, but then his pulse resumed wildly as she placed a leg on either side of him. Straddling him, she partially circled him with her hand and lowered herself just enough to brush against him. They both gasped. Then she sank down the rest of the way, sheathing him deep inside her. The sensation of her squeezing around him was so unbearably pleasurable it was its own kind of torment.

She rocked against him, finding her own rhythm, then made good on her vow not to be gentle, her hips rolling as she slid up and down. He cupped her breasts together and swept his thumbs roughly over the nipples, urging her with his hands to bend down and let him taste her.

Her frantic moans as he suckled sent the pressure pounding through him even closer to detonation. Just as he knew he couldn't hold out any longer, her inner walls contracted and she came with a small scream that was drowned out by the way he called her name when his own body shattered.

Very slowly, his conscious mind returned from incomparable oblivion.

Olivia had collapsed on top of him, and he held her close, unable to imagine letting her run off as she had after the first time they'd made love. Judging from her soft sigh of satisfaction and the way she happily snuggled against him, leaving wouldn't be an issue.

"That was..." She sighed again.

He didn't know if she couldn't think of a word to describe what they'd shared, or if she just didn't have the energy to finish her sentence. He knew he wouldn't have. As he rolled them to their sides, though, he summoned enough energy to languidly kiss her.

She kissed him back, running her fingertips over his chest, back and forth through the light whorls of hair there. Considering the mind-blowing sex they'd just had, he was surprised to feel himself stirring against the softness of her thigh.

Drawing her head back on the pillow, she smiled teasingly. "Why do I get the feeling you aren't ready to drift off to sleep now?"

Tendrils of hair clung to her face, having escaped the sophisticated upsweep she'd started the evening with, and despite her words, her expression was one of hopeful anticipation.

"Sorry, sleep's not in the immediate plans," he told her, utterly unapologetic. "I thought we could make love again. And again, and again."

She propped herself up on one elbow. "I do like a man with ambition."

"Do you? Like me, I mean?" Annoyance ruffled through him when he heard his own ridiculous question.

What was he—seventeen and insecure? Hell, he hadn't been insecure with the opposite sex even when he was in high school, nor did he have a history of following phenomenal lovemaking with relationship analysis. He should be coasting in mindless bliss right about now, yet he couldn't help recalling the times Olivia had seemed rigidly disdainful.

Anything but rigid right now, she gave him a confused smile. "Well, we're naked together. Just how much more friendly did you want me to be?"

He chuckled. "No, you were exactly the right amount of friendly." But although he knew they generated plenty of fire, knew he tripped the same switches in her that she did in him, he was greedy for more. He wanted to know she genuinely enjoyed his company and looked forward to being with him.

"Oh, hell." He laughed suddenly, recalling a question she'd once asked and feeling the joke was very much on him. "I guess what I'm trying to say is, am I someone you would consider for companionship and long talks at the end of the day?" He was one embarrassing question away from being *People*'s Sensitive Man of the Year.

She flushed with pleasure, her face rosy and grinning. "You're not satisfied with just this part?"

"No, I want more." His lips curved in a half smile. "But I am ready to do *this part* again."

Testing his words, she reached below his waist, her fingers curving around his hardening sex. "Oh, my."

He took that as a yes.

13

OLIVIA STOOD beneath the pulsating streams of hot water, letting the shower massage muscles still pleasantly sore from a surfeit of physical activity this weekend. It was Sunday evening, and she had a couple of hours before she was due at Justin's house for dinner. She thought back to very late Friday night, standing in the hotel tub under the spray while Justin washed her hair with a gentleness that belied his size. The tenderness had given way to fervent passion as they'd soaped each other up, touching and teasing until they couldn't take it anymore, He'd carried her as far as the nearest condoms to make love a third time.

With a reluctant sigh, Olivia told herself the prolonged lingering was no good for her skin or her water bill, and she flipped off the faucet. She toweled her body dry and wondered what to wear for their first real date. She'd been oddly touched when he'd invited her to have dinner at his house rather than dining out somewhere less personal, but when she'd accepted the offer, she hadn't realized how much she'd miss him between their late-Saturday-morning checkout and now. Had it only been yesterday afternoon since he'd kissed her, run his hands over her body?

This was the problem with decadent behavior—it was addictive. She'd enjoyed every second of their time together, from how he'd felt inside her, to the intimacy of sleeping in his embrace, to the way he'd made her laugh over breakfast in bed. *It's more than addiction. You're falling in love with him.*

Her breathing shallowed. Love?

Okay, sure, he'd been the first person she'd wanted to tell about her promotion, and she couldn't be near him without wanting to touch him, but... Jeanie had once said that she loved Albert because she could be herself with him; when Olivia was with Justin, she could be an even better version of herself. Of *course* she was in love with him. He was charming and funny, thoughtful in his actions and astounding in bed. He paid her such rapt attention that he blotted out everyone and everything else, seeming content to focus solely on her.

And it was too easy to return that focus, even when they were apart. When they'd kissed goodbye yesterday, she'd told herself she could use the solitude. She'd wanted to get a head start on upcoming assignments and prove that, even though her productivity had lagged last week, she deserved her promotion. Yet she hadn't been able to stop herself from thinking about him, and not just in all the delightful sexual ways.

His surprising pillow talk—the endearing admission that he needed more from her than sex—had melted her completely, binding her to him in an even deeper way than their physical connection. Whether she'd set out to or not, she'd given her heart away. At least her taste in men had finally improved.

She shook her head, amused by the absurdity of soul-searching while she stood naked and chilled in the freesia-scented bathroom. She threw the towel over the hanging wooden rack and tugged on matching sapphire-blue bra and panties. An erotic tingle raced through her as she imagined Justin seeing her in them later.

When she went into her room to pick out clothes, she caught her reflection in the mirror and experienced a moment of déjà vu. Only a few days ago she'd stepped out of her shower into this very room to prepare for a date with another man. So much had changed since then.

She'd changed, thanks in part to Justin's liberating influence. Remarkable how wrong her initial impression of him had been. Instead of being another casually selfish heartbreaker, the man was practically too good to be true.

The thought gave her pause, bringing to mind former flames who'd bruised her heart when they'd turned out to be considerably less than they'd seemed. Only time would tell what was in store for her and Justin. She'd learned from experience that words, even actions, couldn't always be relied on.

Had she finally, almost in spite of herself, tumbled head over heels for someone deserving?

JUSTIN CALLED his shot and took a brief moment to line it up. Too brief. The cue ball rolled obligingly across the green felt surface and followed the purple four into a corner pocket.

"Scratch," Bryan said smugly.

While he watched Bryan reposition the white ball, Justin fought the urge to check his watch. He had plenty of time before Olivia came over...too much, in fact. He couldn't wait to see her.

He and Bryan had agreed to a Sunday afternoon game of eight ball earlier in the week, and Justin hadn't wanted to cancel because he couldn't see explaining the sudden frightening urge to clean his house. Maybe the kitchen wasn't up to his sister Andrea's so-sterile-you-could-perform-surgery chef standards, but he'd seen Bryan's town house and knew his own home was far better than most bachelor pads.

Not that the two-story suburban home would ever feel like a bachelor pad, he mused as Bryan sank two striped balls in rapid succession. With the house having been paid off in the life-insurance settlement, keeping it had been a no-brainer, but it was a lot of room and upkeep for just him. He wasn't sure how Andrea and Lisa would feel about his selling it, though, since they'd lived there most of their lives. This home was a last connection to their parents.

Lisa and Andrea don't have to mow the yard or pay the heating bills.

He brushed away the selfish thought, feeling churlish.

"Sorry things with Hope didn't work out last weekend," Bryan said as he banked the twelve ball off the side. "But that's in the past. You remember my mentioning Michelle? Stewardess Michelle—excuse me, *flight attendant*. I'm going to invite her to your birthday party. The two of you should really hit it off."

His birthday party!

Somewhat preoccupied with other things this week,

Justin had entirely forgotten about the get-together at Bryan's on Thursday. "Actually—"

"This better not be the part where you tell me you don't want a fuss, because, buddy, you're getting one. How many years have you waited for your chance to cut loose?"

"The fuss is fine, but I don't need a date. I..." He hesitated, not sure what to say. How to explain Olivia? "There's a co-worker I think I might bring with me, if she wants to come."

Bryan raised his eyebrows. "When I asked who you were watching the other night, didn't you say you'd just noticed someone from work? Would this be the same lady?"

"My shot." He hoped Bryan would drop the subject while Justin pretended he needed silence to concentrate. As if it mattered—Justin had already fallen irretrievably short of his A game. Conversation with Bryan wasn't what had distracted him, though.

The ball rolled to within millimeters of the designated pocket, but he'd used too much spin to make it. When Justin stepped back, his opponent made no move toward the table. Bryan stood to the side, idly chalking his pool cue.

"So, tell me about this co-worker."

She was as feisty as she was vulnerable, and knowing he'd get to see her made his dream job even better. "She's the Design Supervisor. I've worked with her on a couple of shoots."

Bryan grinned. "Damn. I was kinda hoping she was one of the models. I assume you're inviting her to the party because you want to get somewhere with her?"

With Bryan, there was typically only one pertinent "somewhere," and he didn't need to know Justin and Olivia had already made that trip. Numerous times.

"She's just someone I enjoy being with."

Difficult to say why he felt so defensive. Was he embarrassed that his feelings for Olivia had become so serious in such a short time? Was he worried that Bryan, being Bryan, would high-five him and buy him a beer if Justin admitted what had happened after their last photo shoot? Even though he knew his friend liked women—*really* liked women—and wouldn't mean anything by it, that victor's attitude would rub Justin the wrong way today. Olivia wasn't someone to be bragged about over a pool game.

She's special.

Good thing Bryan wasn't a mind reader. He'd never let Justin live this down. For eight years, the two men had joked about the wild and crazy times that lay ahead when Justin reclaimed his independence, and, not a month after Andrea had left home, he'd gone and fallen for someone. It hadn't been what he was seeking—real relationships required compromise, sacrifice, and he couldn't help feeling he'd sacrificed enough these last few years.

But losing Olivia would be a bigger sacrifice. The woman was smart and sassy, surprising and sexy, and he loved the way she made him feel. He couldn't imagine ever being tired of her company, and he found himself thinking up excuses to stop by her office.

When Bryan won the game, it was an act of mercy, putting Justin out of his misery.

"I'd ask if you wanted to play again," Bryan heckled, "but that would imply you played the first time."

"Sorry. Guess my mind's on other things."

"Other people?" his friend asked shrewdly.

Justin glanced at his watch. "I should really get going, so I guess I'll see you Thursday."

His friend nodded. "I'd say give me a call if you change your mind about Michelle, but something tells me you won't."

OLIVIA STOPPED en route to Justin's house to pick up a bottle of wine. It seemed the polite thing to do, yet as she studied the directions and got farther away from downtown, she realized she just didn't see Justin as the pinot grigio type. She made a second stop, pulling into a gas station long enough to grab a six-pack of beer. Then, feeling only slightly foolish and overanalytical, she got back on the road.

As the sun dipped over the horizon and evening became night, she found Justin's subdivision, thinking to herself how out of character his neighborhood seemed. She lived in a haphazardly furnished apartment that until very recently, she'd shared with a roommate, while Justin, the flirt who had a favorite bar and joked about photographing her nude, lived in suburbia? He owned a two-story brick home with a few oak trees in the front yard.

She couldn't have been more surprised if she'd discovered he lived in a cave. Her understanding was that some bachelors considered them homey, as long as they could hook up a satellite dish.

Parking her car next to his, she experienced another

flutter of excitement at seeing him. She knocked on the front door, then took a moment to smooth her black skirt while she waited for him to answer. The door swung open, and Justin flashed her a smile that mirrored her own anticipation. Then he saw the wine she cradled in one arm and the six-pack swinging from her opposite hand.

He laughed. "Planning to get me drunk and have your wicked way with me?"

Despite the nerves she'd been battling ever since she'd acknowledged how much he meant to her, she flashed a sassy grin. "You're half right."

He ushered her inside, taking both the bottle and the beer and placing them on a small hallway table in the tiled foyer. Then he took her into his arms, his mouth seeking hers.

She was a bit breathless when the kiss ended. "Thanks for inviting me over."

"Your timing is perfect. I just finished making dinner. And by 'make,' I mean phoning in the order for Chinese takeout and opening a bag of salad all by myself. I hope Chinese is okay? I got a ton of food so we'd have different dishes to choose from."

"Chinese is fine," she assured him. "I just hope you aren't stuck with too many leftovers."

"Nah, it'll be fine—leftovers beat cooking. Besides, neither of my sisters liked it much, so I've kind of been glutting myself on it. Whenever I used to suggest Chinese, Lisa would wrinkle her nose and insist man cannot live on MSG alone."

Olivia laughed, following him through the narrow hall that passed the staircase and into a spacious kitchen decorated in ivy-print wallpaper and green surfaces. Adjacent to that was a back living room, home to well-worn furniture and an obscenely large television set. The place was homey, neither pristine nor slovenly, just messy enough to be welcoming.

"Can I take your sweater?" he offered.

She glanced down at the scoop-necked teal sweater she wore buttoned up. "Um, I'm not wearing another top underneath it."

He winked at her. "Why do you think I asked?"

Her laughter eased away any remaining nerves. Once the food arrived, she was able to sit across the round glass-top table and eat without knots in her tummy. They discussed everything from people at work to current events and favorite shows. As they rinsed the plates and refrigerated cardboard pagodas of leftover lo mein, Olivia sipped her second glass of wine, knowing the buzz she felt was due more to Justin's company.

She placed the last of the containers on the top shelf and shut the fridge door. No sooner had she straightened than she realized Justin had finished at the sink and moved behind her. It was like that day at the B and B, when he'd been so close but not quite touching, when she'd wanted to spin around in his arms and kiss him, to hell with the onlookers. Now she could. And did.

His tongue swept inside her mouth, a spark to the kindling of desire already stabbing her. She kissed him with ardent determination, putting all the emotion she'd admitted to herself into her actions. He made a "mmm" of satisfaction and slid his hands just inside the waistband of her skirt to pull her closer.

"Want the quick tour?" he asked between the kisses he placed against her collarbone. "You've already seen the kitchen and downstairs guest bath. Upstairs are just bedrooms and my dark room, but we can worry about those later."

His fingers laced with hers, he led her through the living room, moving quickly toward the doorway on the opposite side. "Den. And this is my bedroom."

He stopped suddenly, and she bumped into him, not that either of them minded. There was a small *click*, then soft light emanated from the lamp on a dated nightstand. Next to it was a bed, made but rumpled, covered by a plaid comforter.

"To the left," he told her, "you'll find the highlight of our tour, The Bed."

Olivia laughed, tugging at his shirt as they fell back to the mattress together. While he kissed her, his hands found the zipper at the back of her skirt and she wiggled her hips, thinking that all tours should end so delightfully.

A thrill shot through her when he reached for the buttons of her top, starting at the bottom and working his way up. Soon, he'd be touching her, and her body throbbed with expectation. They wrestled with fabric and fasteners, their earlier playfulness fading. How was it possible to crave him so much after only one night alone in her big empty bed? Or was it not the missing him, but her newfound acknowledgment that Justin held her heart as well as her body that added the extra level of urgency?

Whatever the reason for it, she didn't feel self-conscious about her need, since his movements echoed the same passion. Soon, the only physical barrier between them was the necessary condom, and Olivia couldn't help feeling—wanting to believe—that there weren't emotional barriers, either. When his gaze briefly met hers, adoration was shining in his eyes.

She'd never felt more desired or more aroused. She wanted to feel him everywhere, take him inside her body until neither of them had anything left to give.

Her hands roamed, one through his soft thick hair, the other gliding over the hard bunched muscles of his shoulder. She gyrated against him, kissing any place she could reach as her foot slid restlessly over the back of his calf. Each sensation from the crisp hair on his legs to the salty taste of his skin telegraphed itself through her body, heightening the sharp tension that gripped her. She had no patience or need for anything but him inside her.

When he thrust into her, her body lifted off the mattress, eagerly joining his. He lowered his mouth to hers, and she kissed him back with mindless passion, unable to focus on anything beyond riding the swells of desire in an earthy, primal rhythm. Despite the intensity of their lovemaking, when her orgasm began building inside her, it still shocked her with its speed and force, obliterating her. Her body buckled.

"Justin. *Oh.*" Her voice echoed off the walls of his bedroom. "Oh, I love you."

As HE COLLAPSED on the bed to hold Olivia, Justin's body hummed with satisfaction. It didn't take long, however, for his thoughts to start spinning in the silence of the room. *I love you.* Her unexpected words, as much as the silky tightness of her body, had driven him over the edge. The only problem was, the second she'd made the declaration, he'd felt her subtle but immediate withdrawal—in the way her breath caught and her face turned slightly away from him.

He knew she hadn't meant to say it, suspected she wanted to take the words back. What he *didn't* know was how to respond. When someone who'd never said the words to you before suddenly cried out "I love you" at the brink of climax, it wasn't always wise to take the comment at face value. Especially when the person so obviously regretted saying it. On a scale of one to awkward, it wasn't as bad as, say, blurting, the wrong name, but still....

Was Olivia embarrassed because she hadn't really intended to say it, or was she worried because she had meant it, but didn't know how he felt? In case of the former, returning the sentiment would be a mistake of the worst kind, but assuming her declaration had been sincere, would she even believe him if he answered in kind?

Maybe his reply should be simple and obvious, but he'd witnessed firsthand Olivia's jaded and skittish view of romance. Her cynicism had been less in evidence after their trip to South Carolina, but he didn't want to run her off now with the wrong reaction. On the other hand, how the hell was he supposed to deduce the right reaction when so little of the blood had yet to return to his brain?

He settled for pressing her close to his chest, squeezing her tightly. "You're amazing, you know that?"

There was an awkward pause before she answered, sounding at least mostly normal, "You're not so bad yourself."

Pulling back, he grinned down into her face. "*That* was 'not so bad'?"

"I was afraid 'earth-shattering' might give you an inflated sense of self-worth."

"No worries on that score. You're good for keeping my ego in check." He lifted her hand from his chest and kissed it. "And you're good for my heart."

"I am?" Her smile was wide, but a little shy, too.

He nodded, aware that what he'd said had barely scraped the surface of his startling feelings for her. But it was enough for now.

14

OLIVIA DROVE to work Monday morning in something of a daze. She'd made several failed attempts before finally leaving Justin's house last night—his kisses goodbye did not inspire a woman to turn away. After they'd finished making love, they'd sat half-dressed in his comfortable living room, enjoying microwaved popcorn and a 007 marathon. Personally, Olivia had always rolled her eyes at James Bond, but Justin considered him some sort of hero.

"How can you admire Bond?" she'd teased. "He's completely one-dimensional. Drinks martinis, chases women and carries fanciful weapons and gadgets."

"Which part of that should I not admire?" When she'd brandished one of the sofa pillows in his direction, he'd grinned. "C'mon, finish watching this one with me, and you'll see what you've been missing."

She still wasn't a Bond fan—don't even get her *started* on *Octopussy*—but spending the evening in the circle of Justin's arms, trading quips into the night, had been worth any lost sleep. Finally, she'd insisted that she needed to get home so she could get up in the morning and prepare for work. When he'd told her she should bring a change of clothes and minimum overnight essentials on future dates, her heart had done cartwheels.

Some men, after an unexpected admission of love from someone they were sleeping with, would have faked their own deaths and changed addresses. Yet Justin had seemed to encourage her feelings, even if he hadn't directly told her his. She chose to take this as a sign that he was health food in chocolate's clothing.

Olivia pulled into her usual parking spot at work, and did an astonished double take at Meg, sitting on the hood of her own car in the neighboring space.

"Well?" Meg demanded, the second Olivia opened her door. "I cannot believe you didn't call me, lady. However, in exchange for many salacious details, I may forgive you."

Salacious details? "Geez, Meg, you want me to draw you a picture?"

"I'd prefer Polaroids."

Laughing, Olivia threw her purse over her shoulder. "I did try to call you once on Saturday night, but I got the machine."

And she'd been relieved. Things between her and Justin were so new, she hadn't quite known how to articulate them in a way that didn't make her sound like a total idiot. Was she crazy, bouncing from her relationship with Sean into love with a man she'd known less than a full month?

But Meg wasn't interested in emotional dissection. She peppered Olivia with questions as they fell in step toward the elevator. "Did you go back to his place Friday, or yours?"

"We didn't make it as far as either of our places," Olivia admitted.

"Ohmigosh! You guys did it in a car?"

"Megan." Despite the elevator being deserted, Olivia shot her rather loud friend a quelling glance. People could probably hear Meg up through the shaft and on the fourth floor. "Ladies don't kiss and tell."

"Dammit." Meg bit her lip, still managing to grin impishly. "I knew there was a reason I couldn't be a lady."

When the two parted ways outside Olivia's office, Meg was threatening to imagine her own naughty details. Chuckling, Olivia went to her desk and booted up her computer. As she waited for e-mail to download, she looked around with a sense of satisfaction. Her last day here in office 461. Steve hadn't wanted her boxing up her belongings before the actual announcement, but this week she needed to pack and get situated in her new office.

"Knock, knock."

Olivia glanced up from her monitor at the sound of Justin's voice, her hormones already zinging through her like tiny caffeinated missiles. "Morning."

He leaned in the doorway, wearing a dark brown shirt and khakis, but in her mind, she saw him shirtless and sexy. Maybe even pantless. In fact—

"Why are you smiling like that?" he asked, his tone playfully wary.

She chuckled, deciding to claim some feminine mystique and just let him wonder. "What brings you up here? Not that I'm unhappy to see you."

"Thought I'd offer you the use of my muscles if you need anything carried." He stepped inside, lowering his voice to a sexy decibel. "Plus, it's difficult to stay downstairs when I know you're just a few floors away.

I've always preferred instant gratification to self-denial."

Since she'd met him, so had she. But she couldn't get into the habit of making out during office hours, especially since her new office—*with* windows, thank you very much—was in a part of the building that got more traffic. "I appreciate the offer, but I have so much to do, and—"

"No problem. I just needed to get this out of my system real quick." He leaned across her desk, kissing her hard. The contact was gone almost immediately, yet it had still been effectively possessive. "I'll be going now. Just call me if you need any help."

"Thanks. Maybe after I get everything organized and boxed...." She snapped her fingers, remembering a purchase she'd made Saturday afternoon, one of the things she'd tried to take care of between their times together. "Could I talk you into helping me move something personal, though? I got a great deal on a sofa from a warehouse that's going out of business. The couch is perfect, but they won't deliver, so if you're free one night this week—"

"Absolutely." His eyes danced with mischief. "You do know it's good luck to 'break in' a new piece of furniture, don't you?"

"Somehow, I'm not thinking you do this by cracking a bottle of champagne across it." She was already turned on by the thought of making love to him again. "I have a dinner meeting with management tonight and a salon appointment Friday evening, but any other night this—"

"Damn." He slumped into one of the chairs across

from her. "I can't believe I didn't mention this earlier...my birthday's Thursday."

"Your birthday?" It was disorienting, after how close she'd felt to him, to realize there were a lot of basic facts about him she didn't know. She didn't even know how old he was.

"My friend Bryan's throwing me a bash for the big three-oh."

Well, that answered at least one question.

"Of course, Bryan considers Arbor Day a reason to party. I meant to ask you when you came over last night, but I kept putting it off, and then you distracted me," he told her with a lazy smile.

At another time, that smile would be sending shivers up her back. "Why 'putting it off'?"

He shrugged, seeming, for a second, uncharacteristically ill at ease. "I guess I wasn't sure you'd have fun."

She recalled the way he'd looked at Hewitt's, laughing and in his element at a crowded club, hanging out with people who oozed sex appeal and confidence. Didn't think she'd have fun, or didn't think she'd *be* fun? She'd been invited to budget meetings by people who sounded more enthusiastic than Justin did.

Maybe he's bummed about turning thirty. Don't be all girlie about this. He wouldn't have asked her if he didn't want her there, it was just that guys didn't hand out engraved invitations. They mentioned stuff when it came to mind, like now. Sean had always informed her of social occasions as though her going with him was an afterthought.

Hmm. Bad comparison.

She gave herself a mental shake—she was no longer the socially awkward outsider. She had a new outlook on life, a new lover, a new promotion.

"I'd love to go! It sounds great." *The new me.*

She just wished she could understand why she felt so much like the old one.

WHEN Justin and Olivia strolled up the sidewalk toward Bryan's town house, they were met by pulsating music. Olivia couldn't make out any words, but she could feel the bass through her pumps.

She glanced at Justin—more handsome than should be legal tonight, in black slacks and a green sweater. "Don't the neighbors complain?"

"The neighbors are always the first people Bry invites," he said with a laugh. "They'll be the ones wandering around trying to figure out who the guest of honor is, since they've never met me. I should also warn you that female guests will probably outnumber the male ones two to one."

Gee, and he'd thought she wouldn't have any fun.

Justin rang the doorbell, and a curvy redhead opened the door, announcing over her shoulder, "Bryan, the birthday boy's here!"

They walked inside, and Olivia's first impression was *white*. Bryan had one of those ultramodern decorating schemes—white fireplace in a white wall, white leather sofa set on a bravely white carpet. The other furniture tended toward sleek black and silver tables and speakers, with just enough art and personal effects to keep a visitor from going snow-blind.

The redhead bounced up to kiss Justin on the cheek,

then turned to Olivia. "If you'd like, I can take your purse and jacket upstairs, throw them on the water bed with everyone else's."

"Thanks." Olivia shrugged out of her lined wool coat, wishing she were whipping it off to reveal something more colorful.

Hopelessly unsure what to wear for this particular event, she'd zipped herself into a flattering sleeveless black dress. She knew it looked good on her and that it was appropriate for most occasions, but now Olivia felt drab. The redhead wore a shimmery gold blouse tied just above her midriff with capri pants that were the same shade, but without the sparkles. And her shoes—you could put an eye out with the heels on those babies.

Dismissing thoughts of what other women were wearing, Olivia made herself grin at her date. "Your friend Bryan must laugh in the face of danger. If I had this color scheme, I'd live in fear of a toppled-over glass of red wine."

Justin leaned down, almost brushing her ear when he whispered, "Don't let the downstairs fool you. I've seen the rest of the place, and the upper level is an undecorated sty."

He straightened just as a handsome dark-haired man reached them. She recognized him as one of the pool players from Hewitt's.

"Justin. Happy birthday, man!" He clapped Justin on the shoulder, then turned to Olivia, lifting her hand and kissing it. "Ah, so here's the lovely reason your pool game's gone to hell lately. Bryan Tanner, ma'am.

When you're finished with this loser, you feel free to give me a call."

"Forget it, Tanner. Olivia's way too good for the likes of you." Justin draped his arm around her, and the small display of possession warmed her to her toes. "Olivia Lockhart, meet Bryan Tanner, networking consultant, longtime friend and general miscreant."

"Nice to meet you." She automatically liked Bryan, not because of his inarguable appeal, but because she sensed genuine affection between the two men.

They followed Bryan into the spacious living room, and he pointed out the wet bar, offering to make them both drinks. Justin was being hailed left and right, from ex-co-workers from Hilliard, people he and Bryan had known in college, and all manner of gorgeous women in strappy dresses. Olivia sternly refused to be jealous—he'd come with her. She tried to keep names straight, but eventually gave up the fight.

She stood to the side sipping her Cosmopolitan while Justin and some of his university alumni relived the details of a significant football game. A man she'd been introduced to earlier caught her eye and approached her.

"So, you work with Justin over at Sweet Nothings? Very cool," he told her with a grin that bordered on smarmy. "It must be very erotic to work in the lingerie business."

He followed his comment with a glance that suggested he was picturing her in something crotchless, and she decided it was a good time to excuse herself to find the rest room. There was a half bath downstairs and two women, a green-eyed brunette and a plump blonde wearing a necklace that could pay Olivia's rent, sat on the carpeted steps of the staircase, waiting their turns. Olivia smiled in greeting, and the brunette eyed her up and down. At least Olivia didn't get the impression the woman was imagining her in racy underwear.

"Aren't you Justin's date?" When Olivia nodded, the brunette sighed. "Oh, you are one lucky gal. I went out with him a few times last year. Too bad it didn't get the chance to become something, no offense. I miss the way he looks at you, you know? Like you're really *there*, like no one else matters."

"Yeah. I, um, I do know what you mean." Olivia just hadn't realized he made everyone else feel the same way. Maybe it had something to do with being a photographer—establishing the contact that made the person on the other side of the camera forget the lights and crew and their own inhibitions. Or maybe it was simply his innate sensuality that made a woman want to believe she was the only one he saw.

The bathroom door swung open, and the brunette stood. It was a good thing she disappeared before Olivia did something she'd regret—like pump the other woman for information on why the relationship had never become anything.

When Olivia rejoined the party, she did a quick visual sweep of the room and didn't find her date. What she did see was the finger-food table that called to her like a siren's song. Two big dietary offenders were nervous eating and social eating, and right now they were ganging up on her.

"If you're looking for Justin," a friendly voice said

from behind her, "he's out on the patio. He asked me if I'd keep an eye out for you."

She turned toward Bryan, glad to be rescued from the call of the chips and dip. "Thanks."

He squinted at her, and she realized his gaze was slightly unfocused. Clearly the imported beer in his hand wasn't his first. "You *are* the girl that was at Hewitt's a couple of Saturdays ago? The one Justin kept watching even though he insisted he wasn't watching anyone?"

She really, really liked their host. "Guilty."

Bryan chuckled. "Man works fast, I'll give him that. I'm thrilled he asked you out. Waited eight years for this."

To date her? She was missing something here. "Eight years?"

"Yeah, to have fun again, live a little, now that he's done raising Andrea and Lisa."

Raising them? She'd known he had younger sisters, but she hadn't been clear on when his parents died. She'd assumed there had been relatives or something... Lord, he'd barely been an adult.

"It must have been hard on him," she said slowly, not wanting to admit this was the first she'd heard of it. Not knowing the date of your boyfriend's birthday was one thing; having no clue how he'd spent the last eight years of his life was another.

"Andy and Lisa are good kids, but...well, take that house for instance. Justin in the 'burbs? One minute he was giving me a run for my money collecting phone numbers at parties, the next he was attending PTA meetings and buying God-only-knows-what female supplies at the grocery store." Bryan shuddered.

Olivia tried not to think too much about the first statement, but she couldn't help agreeing with the basic assessment. She'd thought just earlier this week that Justin's house didn't really suit him. "I guess giving up parties was just the tip of the sacrifices he made?"

She shouldn't be prying, no matter how subtle her inquiries or how willing her new friend was to share the information, but the startling revelation about Justin raising two young women rendered her curiosity insatiable. What Bryan described was completely antithetical to the lifestyle she'd always imagined Justin having.

"The very tip," Bryan agreed with a grimace. "A man's got needs, after all. But he's always said that as soon as Andrea was gone, he'd make up for lost time, sow those wild oats."

Wild oats?

Oh, God. Bryan had been right earlier—Justin *did* work fast. Now that Olivia thought about it, hadn't Andrea only left town a few weeks ago, the very night before Justin kissed Olivia in that elevator? She felt the blood drain from her face, probably because her heart hurt too much to pump properly right now. He was looking to reclaim his bachelorhood and she'd blurted out "I love you"? Small comfort though it was, she was grateful it had only happened the one time.

Whatever her expression was, it sobered Bryan some. "Hey, now, don't pay any attention to my babbling. I've had a few. It's the perk of not having to drive home at the end of the night."

"No, that's all right. I'm fine," she lied, glancing through the sliding glass door, to where Justin was laughing with a group of friends on the patio.

Predominantly female friends.

He couldn't be blamed for that, really, given the male-female ratio at Bryan's shindig. It was a completely different thing than when Sean had flirted with women at parties, she told herself. Still, seeing Justin with his gaggle of admirers made her think of the South Carolina photo shoot—him flirting with Felicia and Stormy and any female who came within eye contact. Hadn't he told her that very night that he deserved some time for himself?

She'd thought when he made the pronouncement, he'd just been another selfish male, but he'd won her over with the way he looked at her, with his thoughtfulness…with the connection she felt when they made love. If he saw their involvement as long-term, though, wouldn't he have mentioned his sisters, told her *something* about the past few years? Olivia's stomach churned. Everything from the timing of their first kiss, immediately following his "liberation," to his interest in different women supported what Bryan had told her. Justin wanted this time to sow some oats.

Too bad she hadn't had the good sense not to be one of them.

JUSTIN FORCED HIMSELF not to wolf down the chocolate cake. It had seemed wrong to leave before now, but he couldn't wait to get Olivia alone. Earlier in the evening, when he'd picked her up, he'd wanted to rush to the part where he took her home…and took her to bed.

Now he just wanted to talk to her, make sure she was all right.

Right before he'd opened presents, she'd told him she was having a minor headache from the liquor but that it was nothing and she didn't want to interrupt his party. Her gift had made him smile—collector's edition 007 DVDs. When he'd moved from presents to cards, most people had laughed at the more often than not bawdy good wishes. Olivia had squirmed, looking as if she regretted staying. Or coming in the first place.

He set down his paper plate, then put his hand on her knee. Was he crazy, or did she actually flinch? "Ready to go? I say we make a run for it."

Her smile was halfhearted. Possibly even quarter-hearted. "It's your birthday. We can go if you're ready, or stay if you want."

No, he was definitely getting her out of here. They had about a fifteen-minute drive, and he planned to find out if there was more bothering her than a supposed headache.

He rose from the white ottoman. "I'll run upstairs and get your coat. I could send you, but you wouldn't be able to navigate the clutter. I'm pretty sure Hoffa's actually up there somewhere."

Not even a fraction of a smile this time. Well, it hadn't been that funny, but he was surprised she didn't humor him, what with it being his birthday and all.

Taking the stairs two at a time, he wondered if he'd ignored her tonight. These were his friends, and maybe she'd felt out of place.

He'd just lifted Olivia's jacket from the heap on the bed when Bryan appeared in the doorway.

"Justin. Hold up, buddy. I needed to tell you something."

His friend's tone, while not dire, was pretty somber for a confirmed party animal who'd been playing bartender all night, mostly to a room full of gorgeous women.

"Tell me what?"

"Earlier, when you were on the patio, Olivia and I talked for a few minutes...."

Given Bryan's reluctance to blurt out whatever he'd come up here to say and Olivia's less than sparkly mood, Justin guessed that something had gone wrong. He knew that Bryan was way too good a friend ever to hit on his date, but it wouldn't be the first time he'd inadvertently offended a woman.

"What did you say to her?"

"Nothing I didn't think she already knew. You never told her about Andrea and Lisa?"

A tingle of foreboding went through him. "Told her what, exactly? She knows I have sisters."

"Did she know you raised them?"

"No." But he didn't really see why that would upset her too badly. It just wasn't something he liked to talk about—omitting it hadn't been anything personal.

"I, ah, I also might have mentioned The Plan." Bryan rocked back on his heels, sheepishly addressing the carpet. "You know, the one about you getting your freedom back and playing the field."

"You *what?*" This was the last thing she needed to hear, on top of her ex sleeping around.

"It just sort of slipped out. I told her I didn't really mean it, that it was the beer talking, but...you may have some damage control to do."

Some? He didn't even know where to begin. In the last few weeks, Olivia had transformed from someone wary about love, fresh from a betrayal of trust, to a woman who generously gave her laughter and her body. And, unless he was mistaken, her love.

He'd tell her how he felt tonight. He just hoped she hadn't withdrawn so far into her protective shell that she wouldn't want to hear it.

15

OLIVIA HUDDLED into her coat as they walked to Justin's car, but she wasn't really surprised when it didn't make her feel warmer. He opened her door for her, and she was sure he noticed how stiff her body was. How she took pains not to brush against him.

She watched him walk around the car to his side, admiring his graceful stride despite her mood. Every move the man made was raw poetry. Was it any wonder she'd fallen under his spell?

Maybe she was overreacting to be this upset, but she felt brittle, as if the wrong touch could shatter her. She'd been so sure she'd got it right this time, that she'd fallen for the one man who...

"It's okay, you know," Justin said softly. "Bryan told me what he said. I figure you're pissed."

She shook her head. "I'm not angry, exactly. We didn't make each other any promises. I was more surprised than anything else." That was as truthful as her stinging pride would allow.

"I guess I could've mentioned my sisters earlier. I have trouble discussing it all," he admitted. "How can I gripe about having to take them to soccer practice or sit through games, considering all they've been through? I'd like to think I'm not truly selfish enough to hold the house or a slow love life against them."

"It's okay to have your own wants," she said softly. "Just don't read too much into what Bryan said."

"Tell me the truth." She turned to face him, even though his eyes were on traffic. "Did you not spend the last eight years wishing your life was different, making plans to—"

"Yeah. I did. He didn't lie, but things changed when I met you."

"I changed what you wanted?"

Right. She, whose boyfriends had been known to jump into bed with the first willing female the second her back was turned, had in a matter of weeks changed an eight-year desire and his entire outlook on life. Made sense.

"Yes. No. You made me see that what I thought I wanted wasn't. What I want is what we have. I love you."

The unexpected words sliced through her. For a second, they filled her with joy, but tonight had laid open too many raw wounds and insecurities for her to feel confident in his declaration. "What if you're wrong?"

"About loving you? I'm a grown man, Olivia, not an infatuated teenager."

She could attest to the grown man part. "This, us, is still new and exciting. Once the newness wears off—"

"What about when it wears off for you?" he countered. "You won't love me four months from now?"

Dammit. When he hadn't said anything before, she'd hoped she was going to get away scot-free with her passion-induced admission. Passion-induced, but truth-filled.

"I'm not the one who wasn't able to order Chinese food for eight years."

His gaze shot from the road to her, just long enough to look at her as though she were crazy. "I have no idea what you're talking about."

"You said Sunday that Andrea and Lisa didn't like Chinese and now you can't get enough of it. I think you said you were glutting yourself on it. What about dates? I'll bet you didn't have enough of those. If we stay together, are you going to resent me? Wish you hadn't given up your chance at sowing oats so quickly?"

"That's not going to happen. I'm not twenty-two anymore."

When she didn't say anything, he exhaled in frustration. "You're asking for evidence I can't give. What am I supposed to do to make you trust in my emotions tomorrow or next week or next month?"

Olivia didn't have an answer for that. She wanted to believe him, wanted to love him without reservations, more than she ever had with anyone else she'd known. And that terrified her. She'd freely admitted to Meg that she'd never loved Sean, yet his betrayal had still taken its toll. What would losing Justin do to her, if she forced herself to take his words on faith, only to be proven wrong? Again.

The strained silence had grown deafening by the time Justin turned his car into the parking lot of her apartment complex.

"Don't do this," he told her. "I know you. I might not have all the details, but I know sometimes you hide from things. You don't have to run from this."

She stiffened. "I know you, too, Justin. I know you look up to Bryan, a confirmed playboy if I ever met one, and a fictional spy who sleeps with a parade of women. I know you like spontaneity and socializing. I know you flirt. You'd either get bored with me, or I'd get suspicious of you. Or both."

He followed her out of the car, up the walkway to her apartment. "Olivia—"

"From what you said earlier, you had to struggle against resenting your sisters, even though your feelings are completely understandable. I can't stand the thought of you resenting me.

"I'm sorry," she said as she opened the door to her apartment. "I—I care about you too much already, and if it didn't work out...I'm sorry. I just can't."

TELLING HERSELF she could be just as productive working at home as surrounded by the distractions of the office, Olivia took the cowardly way out and called in sick Friday.

It wasn't untrue—she was heartsick. She sent a brief e-mail to Meg, not going into gory detail, but making it clear she and Justin were no more. Other than that, there'd been no contact with anyone else at Sweet Nothings. When the doorbell rang shortly after five, her heart stopped for a second, and her fingers curled into the armrest of her chair.

Justin hadn't tried to call her, which was just as well, really, but what if that was because he'd decided to talk to her in person?

The doorbell chimed again. "You in there, Olivia? It's me. I brought you something."

Meg. Touched by her friend's thoughtfulness, Olivia answered the door with her tissue box in hand. "Hi."

"Oh, honey." Meg sighed. "You look like hell."

Olivia's laugh was sniffly. "Come on in, anyway." Oddly, she couldn't recall shedding a single tear after she'd found Sean, whom she'd dated longer than she'd even known Justin, in the ultimate act of disloyalty.

"Here." Meg handed her a paper sack that was warm to the touch. "I don't have your recipe so I just picked you up some soup at the deli. I know you're not sick in the traditional sense, but I thought it might help."

"Thanks." The two women went into the kitchen, where Olivia pulled down just one bowl after Meg shook her head to indicate she didn't want anything.

"Would it help if I told you he looked awful today, too?" Meg asked from her seat at the table.

Yes. "No. The man should still be celebrating his birthday, his…his independence. I don't want him to be miserable." Much.

"Do you want to talk about it?"

"I should." Olivia poured herself a glass of water and managed to carry that and the piping-hot bowl of soup to the table without spilling anything. "I can't work from home every day, and how am I going to face him if I can't even discuss him?"

Why hadn't she listened to herself when she'd maintained it would be a bad idea to get involved with someone from Sweet Nothings? Olivia lifted a spoonful of the soup, but delicious as it was, its comforting properties were no match for the pain of losing Justin.

"Oh, Meg. I just never learn. I keep saying I'm not

going to repeat my mistakes and fall for the wrong
men, but—"

"When did he become the wrong man? The two of
you have been grinning idiots all week. I mean *idiot* in
the good way."

"Yeah, but that was before I found out the truth—"

"That he's married? Has a felony record? Kicks pup-
pies? I gotta tell you, I'm not sure I understand why his
raising his sisters translates to you losing someone who
made you so happy."

"Relationships don't work when only one person is
happy. And after what Bryan told me last night, I don't
see how Justin could stay happy for long."

"Bryan." Meg snorted. "If I ever get introduced to
the man, I'm going to wring his neck. Forget what he
told you, what did Justin say?"

"Th-that he…" The sob caught in her throat, becoming a hiccup. "That he loved me."

"And this is bad because…?"

"Meg, I wasn't able to keep the interest of guys who
claimed to want a relationship in the first place, much
less a man who's been swearing to himself he'll make
up for eight years of lost bachelorhood." She ran her
hand through her unkempt hair. "Even if he was telling the truth, and our affair *wasn't* about oats, how
long do you think we could last before he realized
what I'd cheated him out of, the freedom he waited almost a decade to get? If I'm going to lose him, I'd rather
do it now."

"You don't think the man is responsible enough to
choose what he wants for himself?"

"I think he's been a grown-up since before he was

ready, and he deserves some time off from adult responsibility."

Meg laughed. "We all deserve some time off from adult responsibility. That doesn't mean we're gonna get it. Life goes on. Best we can hope for is the right person to share everything with. Sounds to me like you and Justin were lucky enough to find that, so why are you here slurping down soup with me instead of having fantastic make-up sex with him?"

The thought of never again being in bed with him had fresh tears pricking her eyes. "Meg, you don't understand."

"Yeah. I do. You know how many times I've heard you say you've made bad decisions about guys? I don't think this is about Justin. I think it's about your fear of getting hurt. And much as I love you, Olivia, I think this is the first truly dumb decision you've made about a guy since I've known you."

An hour after Meg's departure, Olivia was staring at the television, but the only dialogue she heard was her friend's well-meaning accusation still ringing in her ears.

Am I making a dumb decision?

She wanted to trust in what she felt for Justin, wanted to trust what he claimed to feel for her. But in the past— Then again, Justin wasn't any of those men. And she wasn't the same woman. She'd realized that recently. She *could* follow her instincts, be bold and unrestrained.

So, why wasn't she doing that now? Doing so had landed her the promotion she'd wanted since January, had landed her Justin, even though she'd screwed that up last night by retreating to her old ways. Hiding, he'd said.

He wasn't wrong.

She could recall too many times in her life when she'd wanted to be invisible, but it had felt damn good to walk into that hotel ballroom last Friday night and have heads turn. Justin talked about taking pictures, making people see things the way he did. When he looked at her, did he see someone as bold and unrestrained as she felt when he touched her—or someone who let past hurts define her future?

More importantly, if she went and looked in the mirror right now, who would she see?

JUSTIN MADE a mad dash for the kitchen phone when it rang Friday night, even though he knew chances were slim it would be Olivia.

"Hello?"

"Hey," Bryan said. "Thought I'd better call to see if you were still speaking to me."

"I'm speaking to you. I just can't guarantee some of the words won't be of the four-letter variety," he said with no real anger in his tone.

His friend sighed. "I guess I ruined the rest of your evening last night? On your birthday, no less. I suck."

Justin didn't disagree.

"I'm sure the two of you will work it out." Bryan's words actually seemed to stem from conviction, rather than guilt. "When you first came in last night, I noticed the way you two look at each other. It wasn't just the hots. I know the hots. It was something that almost made me wish…never mind. That's crazy talk. But the part about you and Olivia working it out was true."

How ironic that Bryan had sounded almost wistful, after all the times Justin had wished his life were as pleasurable and uncomplicated as his friend's. But "uncomplicated" was no match for the sheer need Justin felt to be in Olivia's company. He loved being with her, loved *her*, whether she wanted to accept that or not.

"You want to grab a beer?" Bryan invited.

Justin laughed. "Now I know you feel bad. You're telling me you'd cancel your date tonight with Michelle the flight attendant?"

"I was hoping you'd just say no, and I could go on record as making the offer."

Laughing again, Justin told his to go enjoy a guilt-free evening. At least one of them should have fun.

No sooner had he hung up the phone than the doorbell rang. Since he knew it wasn't Bryan coming to check on him and he hadn't phoned in an order for dinner yet, it was probably a door-to-door solicitor. Conversing with a vacuum-cleaner salesman wouldn't be any worse than wallowing in self-pity.

He opened the door, his greeting frozen in his throat at the vision on his front porch. No door-to-door salesman had ever looked like this.

Olivia stood in her trench coat, her eyes dramatic and soulful. She'd cut her hair—it was chin-length now, styled in jagged layers that gave her an edgy modern appearance but somehow also looked soft, wispy. He was so caught off guard by her presence here and her altered appearance, it took him a moment to realize they were at eye level.

He looked down to see a pair of dark green shoes with pointed toes and stiletto heels.

"May I come in?" she asked quietly.

Instead of waiting for an answer, she took his shell-shocked silence as a yes and stepped past him.

"I didn't expect to see you." He shut the door. Unable to resist touching her, he threaded his fingers through the soft feathery layers of her new hairstyle, then stopped them at the side of her face. "This is different. Perfect for you, but I can't believe you got it all cut off."

It really was perfect for her—as if this had been the real Olivia on the inside, and she'd waited until now to spring it on everyone else.

"I've worn it long since high school—I think someone told me once it was slimming—and it became something else I hid behind." Her breathing was uneven, but her tone was confident. "No more hiding. You were right, and I was wrong, but don't expect that I'll always be saying that after our disagreements."

He blinked, feeling as though they'd somehow missed a crucial step, like a scratched compact disc that skips, going discordantly from one part of the song to the next without transition. "Say that again?"

"You were right. I was wrong." She met his gaze. "I do love you."

His entire being thrummed with emotion. This was probably where he should sweep her into his arms and kiss her. God knows he wanted to, but he couldn't yet.

"You love me enough to believe I love you?" he

asked, needing her confidence once and for all in what they shared. "Because having to prove myself every time Bryan puts his foot in his mouth would be exhausting. For the past few years, after having responsibility thrust on me, I did think I wanted freedom, but all I really wanted was freedom of choice. I'm not going to resent you, Olivia. I *choose* you."

She swallowed, the depth of feeling in her gaze matching his own. "I believe you."

Good, then he could kiss her now. He sealed his mouth over hers, backing her against the foyer wall. His hand went to the belt on her jacket, releasing the leather knot.

"I don't suppose you're naked under there?" Could one man be so lucky?

"Not entirely." She laughed. "Although you do bring out my wilder tendencies."

He slid her jacket off her shoulders and swallowed at the sight of her in a bustier he'd pointed out this week in the catalog. "Nice."

"I understand this is the part where we have fantastic make-up sex." Her naughty tone didn't hide the vulnerability in her eyes. "That is, if we're made up now? I am sorry for last night. I'm a little shaky about feeling this way, and what Bryan told me gave me the perfect excuse to bail. I haven't had a lot of luck with love."

"Yes, but that was before me." He raised an eyebrow. "I'm extraordinarily gifted."

She kissed his jaw, then lowered her head, biting lightly at the side of his neck. "Very true. Do you know what else you are?"

"Aroused." He tugged her gently toward the back of the house.

"A caramel-covered apple," she said as they passed through the living room. "I used to think you were chocolate, but it turns out that beneath the decadent exterior, you really are good for me...did I mentioned how much I enjoy taking my time and thoroughly licking off all the caramel?"

Justin groaned at the thought of Olivia running her tongue over him and pulled her down on the couch, plunging his hands into her short hair and kissing her deeply. "I was planning to take you to bed, but we're not going to make it that far."

"What about making love on a beach?" she asked as she removed his shirt. "I have this vacation coming up, to the lovely island of Kaokara..."

He wasn't sure they'd get out of the hotel room long enough to see much of the island, but if Olivia was going to be there, it was where he wanted to be.

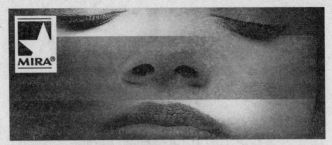

"Twisted villains, dangerous secrets...irresistible."
—*Booklist*

New York Times Bestselling Author

STELLA
CAMERON

Just weeks after inheriting Rosebank, a once-magnificent Louisiana plantation, David Patin was killed in a mysterious fire, leaving his daughter, Vivian, almost bankrupt. With few options remaining, Vivian decides to restore the family fortunes by turning Rosebank into a resort hotel.

Vivan's dream becomes a nightmare when she finds the family's lawyer dead on the sprawling grounds of the estate. Suddenly Vivian begins to wonder if her father's death was really an accident...and if the entire Patin family is marked for murder.

Rosebank is not in Sheriff Spike Devol's jurisdiction, but Vivian, fed up with the corrupt local police, asks him for unofficial help. The instant attraction between them leaves Spike reluctant to get involved—until another shocking murder occurs and it seems that Vivian will be the next victim.

kiss them goodbye

"Cameron returns to the wonderfully atmospheric Louisiana setting...for her latest sexy-gritty, compellingly readable tale of romantic suspense."—*Booklist*

Available the first week of October 2004,
wherever paperbacks are sold!

The world's bestselling romance series.

HARLEQUIN®
Presents

Seduction and Passion Guaranteed!

THEPRINCESSBRIDES

For duty, for money…for passion!

Discover a thrilling new trilogy from a rising star of Harlequin Presents®, Jane Porter!

Meet the Royals…

Chantal, Nicolette and Joelle are members of the blue-blooded Ducasse family. Step inside their sophisticated and glamorous world and watch as these beautiful princesses find they have to marry three international playboys—for duty, for money… and definitely for passion!

Don't miss

THE SULTAN'S BOUGHT BRIDE (#2418)
September 2004

THE GREEK'S ROYAL MISTRESS (#2424)
October 2004

THE ITALIAN'S VIRGIN PRINCESS (#2430)
November 2004

Pick up a Harlequin Presents® novel and you will enter a world of spine-tingling passion and provocative, tantalizing romance!

Available wherever Harlequin books are sold.

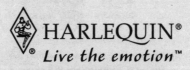

HARLEQUIN®
Live the emotion™

www.eHarlequin.com

On sale now

girls' night in

21 of today's hottest
female authors
1 fabulous short-story collection
And all for a good cause.

Featuring *New York Times* bestselling authors

Jennifer Weiner (author of *Good in Bed*),
Sophie Kinsella (author of *Confessions of a Shopaholic*),
Meg Cabot (author of *The Princess Diaries*)

Net proceeds to benefit War Child, a network of organizations
dedicated to helping children affected by war.

Also featuring bestselling authors...

Carole Matthews, Sarah Mlynowski, Isabel Wolff, Lynda Curnyn,
Chris Manby, Alisa Valdes-Rodriguez, Jill A. Davis, Megan McCafferty,
Emily Barr, Jessica Adams, Lisa Jewell, Lauren Henderson,
Stella Duffy, Jenny Colgan, Anna Maxted, Adèle Lang,
Marian Keyes and Louise Bagshawe

RED
DRESS
INK ™

www.RedDressInk.com   www.WarChildusa.org

Available wherever trade paperbacks are sold.

™ is a trademark of the publisher.
The War Child logo is the registered trademark of War Child.

RDIGNIMMR